The Strange Adventures of Mr. Middleton

Wardon Allan Curtis

Alpha Editions

This edition published in 2024

ISBN : 9789362999337

Design and Setting By
Alpha Editions
www.alphaedis.com
Email - info@alphaedis.com

As per information held with us this book is in Public Domain.
This book is a reproduction of an important historical work. Alpha Editions uses the best technology to reproduce historical work in the same manner it was first published to preserve its original nature. Any marks or number seen are left intentionally to preserve its true form.

Contents

The Manner in Which Mr. Edward Middleton Encounters the Emir Achmed Ben Daoud. ....- 1 -

The Adventure of the Virtuous Spinster. ....- 6 -

What Befell Mr. Middleton Because of the Second Gift of the Emir. ....- 12 -

The Adventure of William Hicks. ....- 15 -

What Befell Mr. Middleton Because of the Third Gift of the Emir. ....- 22 -

The Adventure of Norah Sullivan and the Student of Heredity. ....- 31 -

What Befell Mr. Middleton Because of the Fourth Gift of the Emir. ....- 38 -

The Pleasant Adventures of Dr. McDill. ....- 47 -

What Befell Mr. Middleton Because of the Fifth Gift of the Emir. ....- 59 -

The Adventure of Miss Clarissa Dawson. ....- 65 -

What Befell Mr. Middleton Because of the Sixth Gift of the Emir. ....- 81 -

The Unpleasant Adventure of the Faithless Woman. ....- 91 -

What Befell Mr. Middleton Because of the Seventh Gift of the Emir. ....- 98 -

The Adventure of Achmed Ben Daoud. ....- 114 -

What Befell Mr. Middleton Because of the Eighth and Last Gift of the Emir...............................- 128 -

THE MANNER IN WHICH MR. EDWARD MIDDLETON ENCOUNTERS THE EMIR ACHMED BEN DAOUD.

IT WAS a lowering and gloomy night in the early part of the present century. Mr. Edward Middleton, a gallant youth, who had but lately passed his twenty-third year, was faring northward along the southern part of that famous avenue of commerce, Clark Street, in the city of Chicago, wending his way toward the emporium of Mr. Marks Cohen. Suddenly the rain which the cloudy heaven had been promising for many hours, began to descend in great scattered drops that presaged a heavy shower. Mr. Middleton hastened his steps. It was possible that if the dress-suit he wore, hired for the occasion of the wedding of his friend, Mr. Chauncey Stackelberg, should become imbued with moisture in the shower that now seemed imminent, Mr. Cohen, of whom he had hired the suit, would not add to the modicum agreed upon, a charge for pressing it. But if his own suit for everyday wear, which he was carrying under his arm with the purpose of putting it on at good Mr. Cohen's establishment, should become wet, that would be a serious matter. It was, in fact, his only suit and that will explain the anxiety with which he scanned the heavens. Suddenly, Pluvius unloosed all the fountains of the sky, and with scarcely a thought whither he was going, Mr. Middleton darted into the first haven of refuge, a little shop he happened to be just passing. As the door closed behind him with the tinkle of a bell in some remote recess, for the first time he realized that the place he had entered was utterly dark. His ears, straining to their uttermost to make compensation for the inability of his eyes to be of service to him in this juncture, could no more than inform him that the place was utterly silent. But to his nose came the powerful fragrance of strange foreign aromas such as he had never had experience of before,— which, heavy and oppressive in their cloying perfume, seemed the very breath of mystery. All traffic had ceased without, as the night was well advanced and the rain beat so heavily that the few whom business or pleasure had called abroad at that hour, had sought shelter. But though the rain now fell with a steady roar, Mr. Middleton, perturbed by a nameless disquiet, was about to rush forth into the tempest and seek other shelter, when a door burst open and, outlined against a glare of light, stood a gigantic man who said in a deep, low voice that seemed to pervade every corner of the room and cause the air to shake in slow vibrations, "Salaam aleikoom!" Which being repeated again, Mr. Middleton replied:

"I do not understand the German language."

A low, musical laugh greeted this remark and the laugh resolving itself into a low, musical voice that bade him enter, Mr. Middleton found himself in a small boudoir of oriental magnificence, facing a young man in the costume of the Moslem nations, who sat cross-legged upon a divan smoking a narghileh. He was of perhaps twenty-six, somewhat slight, but elegant of person. His face, extremely handsome, betokened that he was a man of intelligence and sensibility. Two brilliant, sparkling eyes illumined his countenance and the curl of his carmine lips was that of one who while kind—without condescension and the odiousness of patronage—to all whom the mischance of fate had made his inferiors in fortune, would not bend the fawning knee to any whom the world calls great. Behind him stood a giant blackamore, he of the voice that had saluted Mr. Middleton. The blackamore was dressed in crimson silk sparkling with an array of gold lace, but his immense turban was snowy white. Against his shoulder reposed a great glittering scimetar and a dozen silver-mounted pistols and poniards were thrust in his sash.

Presently the young man removed the golden mouth-piece of the narghileh from his lips and regarding Mr. Middleton fixedly, remarked:

"There is but one God and Mohammed is his Prophet."

Now this was not the doctrine Mr. Middleton had been taught in the Methodist Sunday School in Janesville, Wisconsin, but disliking to dispute with one so engaging as the handsome Moslem, and having read in a book of etiquette that it was very ill mannered to indulge in theological controversy and, moreover, being conscious of the presence of the blackamore with the glittering scimetar, he began to make his excuses for an immediate departure. But the Moslem would not hear to this.

"Mesrour will bear your garments to Mr. Cohen. From your visage, I judge you to be a person I wish to know. I take you to be endowed with probity, discretion, and valor, and not without wit, good taste, and good manners. Mesrour, relieve the gentleman of his burden."

Whereupon Mr. Middleton was compelled to state that it was the garment on his back that was to go to Mr. Cohen, though he feared this confession would cause him to fall in the estimation of the Moslem. But the stranger relaxed none of his deference at this intimation that Mr. Middleton was not a person of consequence.

"Mesrour, take two sequins from the ebony chest. The price the extortionate tailor charges, is some thirty piastres. Bring back the change and a receipt."

"Salaam, effendim!" and Mesrour bowed until the crown of his head was presented toward his master, together with the palms of his hands, and in this posture backed from the room, leaving Mr. Middleton speculating upon the wonder and alarm little Mr. Cohen would experience at beholding the gigantic Nubian in all his outlandish panoply. While changing the dress suit for his street wear, from a back room came the sound of the blackamore moving about, chanting that weird refrain, tumpty, tumpty, tum—tum; tumpty, tumpty, tum—tum; which from Mesopotamia to the Pillars of Hercules, from the time of Ishmael to the present, has been the song of the sons of the desert. What was his surprise when the blackamore emerged. Gone were his turban, his flowing trousers, his scimetar, pistols, and poniards. He had on a long yellow mackintosh, which did not, however, conceal a pair of black and white checked pantaloons, a red tie, and green vest, from each upper pocket of which projected an ivory-handled razor.

"Don't forget the change, Mesrour."

"No indeed, boss," replied the blackamore, whistling "Mah Tiger Lily," as he departed.

The Moslem provided Mr. Middleton with one of those pipes which in various parts of the Orient are known as narghilehs, hubble-bubbles, or hookabadours, and seeing his guest entirely at his ease, without ado began as follows:

"My name is Achmed Ben Daoud, and I am hereditary emir of the tribe of Al-Yam, which ranges on the border of that fortunate part of the Arabian peninsular known as Arabia the Happy. My youngest brother, Ismail, desirous of seeing the world, went to the court of Oman, where struck by his inimitable skill in narration, the imam installed him as royal story-teller. But having in the space of a year exhausted his stock of stories, the imam, who is blessed with an excellent memory, discovering that he was telling the same stories over again, shut him up in a tower constructed of vermilion stone quarried on the upper waters of the great river Euphrates. There my poor brother is to stay until he can invent a new stock of stories, but being utterly devoid of invention, only death or relenting upon the part of the imam could release him. Hearing of his plight, I went to the imam with the proposition that I seek out some other story-teller and that upon bringing him to Muscat, my brother be released. But the imam exclaimed that he was tired of tales of genii and magicians, of enchantments and spells, devils, dragons, and rocs.

"'These things are too common, too everyday. Go to the country of the Franks and bring me a story-teller who shall tell me tales of far nations, and I will release Ismail, and load him with treasure.'

"'My Lord,' said I, 'peradventure no Frank story-teller will come. To guard against such eventuality, I will myself go to the lands of the Franks, there to learn of adventures worthy the ear of your highness. This I will do that my brother may be released from the vermilion tower.'

"'Do this, and I will give him the vermilion tower and make him grand vizier of the dominions of Oman.'

"As hereditary emir of the tribe of Al-Yam, I am prince of a considerable population. My revenues are sufficient to support life becomingly. But desiring to escape attention, and moreover, feeling that I could better get in touch with all classes of the population, I have established here in Chicago a small bazaar for the sale of frankincense and myrrh, the balsam of Hadramaut and attar of roses from the vales of Nejd, coffee of Mocha—which is in Arabia the Happy—dates from Hedjaz, together with ornaments made from wood grown in Mecca and Medina. Such is my stock in trade. By day, Mesrour and I dress like Feringhis. But at night, it pleases us to cast aside the stiff garb of the infidel for the flowing garments of my native land. Mesrour then delights to make the obeisances my rank deserves, but which in the presence of the giaours would excite mocking laughter. I have prospered. I have made acquaintances and have learned of many adventures. But I have made no friends. I have been much prepossessed by your bearing and feel that I would like to have you for a friend. I am also desirous of observing the effect of the tales of adventure I have been collecting. I need to acquire skill in the art of narration, and accordingly, I must have someone to tell them to, a person whose complaisance will cause him to overlook the faults of a novice. I am exceedingly anxious to have the distinguished honor of your company and if you have any evenings when you are at leisure, I should be only too glad to have you spend them here."

"I can come this day week," said Mr. Middleton.

"So be it. On that occasion I will tell you the tale of The Adventure of the Virtuous Spinster. I have not asked you your calling in life, for I am utterly without curiosity——"

"I am a clerk in a law office," said Mr. Middleton, quickly, "where I perform certain tasks and at the same time study law, and it is my hope to be soon admitted to the bar."

Prince Achmed regarded him earnestly for a moment, and then withdrew to return with a sandalwood case in his hands. This he opened to disclose a leathern-bound volume. Upon the cover was stamped a great gilt monogram of letters in some strange language. The edges were stained a brilliant and peculiarly vivid green. The pages were of fine pearl-colored vellum, covered with strange characters in black. Each chapter began with a great red initial surrounded by an illuminated design of many colored arabesques. It was indeed a volume to cause a book-lover to cry out with joy.

"Here is all the law man needs, the sacred Koran. Here is the beginning and end of law, the source of regulations that ensure righteous conduct, the precepts of Mohammed, prophet of Allah. If other laws agree with those of the Koran, they are needless. If they disagree, they are evil. Study this guide of life, my friend, and there will be no need to worry your brain with tomes of the presumptuous wights who from their own imaginings dare attempt to dictate laws and impiously substitute them for the laws revealed to Mohammed from on high. Accept this gift and study it."

With the sandalwood case containing the precious volume of the law under his arm, Mr. Middleton departed. After the lapse of three days, finding no immediate prospect of learning the Arabic language, and fearful of offending Prince Achmed if he returned the book, and having no possible use for it, he took it to a bibliophile, who exclaiming that it was the handiwork of a Mohammedan monastery of Damascus and bore on the cover the monogram of the fifth Fatimite caliph, and was therefore a thousand years old, he told Mr. Middleton that though it was worth much more, he could offer him but five hundred dollars, which sum the astonished friend of Achmed received in a daze, and departed to invest in a well located lot in a new suburb. Having no use for the sandalwood case after the Koran had been disposed of, he presented it to a young lady of Englewood as a receptacle for handkerchiefs.

Mr. Middleton said nothing of these transactions when on the appointed evening he once more sat in the presence of the urbane prince of the tribe of Al-Yam. Having handed him a bowl of delicately flavored sherbet, Achmed began to narrate The Adventure of the Virtuous Spinster.

THE ADVENTURE OF THE VIRTUOUS SPINSTER.

MISS ALMIRA JOHNSON was a virtuous spinster, aged thirty-nine, who lived in a highly respectable boarding-house on the north side. Her days she spent in keeping the books of a large leather firm, in an office which she shared with two male clerks who were married, and a red-headed boy of sixteen, who was small for his age.

On the evening when my tale begins, Miss Almira, tastefully attired for her night's rest in a white nightgown trimmed with blue lace, was peeping under the bed for the ever-possible man, the nightly rite preliminary to her prayers. She fell back gasping in a vain attempt to scream, but not a sound could she give vent to. The precaution of years had been justified. There lay a man! He was habited in a very genteel frock-suit, patent-leather shoes, and although it must have caused him some inconvenience in his recumbent position, upon his head was a correct plug hat. The elegance and respectability of his garb somewhat reassured Miss Almira, who was unable to believe that one so apparelled could have secreted himself under her bed for an evil purpose, when a new fear seized her, for arguing from this assumption, she concluded he must have been placed there by others and was, in short, dead. Whereupon, having to some degree recovered possession of herself, she was opening her mouth to scream at this new terror, when the man spoke.

"Listen before you scream, I pray thee, beauteous lady, darling of my life, pearl of my desires, star of my hopes."

The strangeness of the address and the unaccustomed epithets caused Miss Almira to forbear, for she could not hear what he had to say and scream at the same time, and, moreover, she remembered how twenty years before, Jake Long had fled, never to return to her side, when after telling her she was the sweetest thing in the world, she had screamed as his arms clasped about her in a bearish hug.

"Fair lady, ornament of your sex, hear the words of your ardent admirer before you blast his hopes."

As he uttered these words, the stranger extricated himself from his undignified position and sat down in a rocking chair before the bureau. Miss Almira was more than ever prepossessed as she saw he wore white kid gloves and that in his shirt front gleamed a large diamond. He removed his hat, disclosing a heavy crop of black hair. He had blue eyes and a strong, clean-shaven face.

"For some time I have observed you and wondered how I was to realize my fondest hopes and make your acquaintance. All day you are in the office, where the two married men and the red-headed boy are always de trop. My employment is of a nature that takes me out nights. In fact, I teach a night school for Italians. To-day being an Italian holiday and so no school, and as there is a possibility I shall soon leave the city for an extended season, I have been unable to devise any other means of declaring myself before the time for my departure. Pray pardon me for the abruptness and importunity of my declaration, pray forgive me for the unusual way which I have taken to secure an interview alone with you. But if you only knew the ardor of my love, my impatience—oh, would that our union could be effected this very night!"

Ravished by the elegance of the stranger both in his outward seeming and his converse, melted by the warmth of a romantic devotion almost unknown in these degenerate days, though common enough of yore, Miss Almira paused a moment in the proud compliance of one about to gladly bestow an inestimable, but hardly hoped-for gift, and crying, "It can be done, it shall be done," threw herself into the cavalier's arms.

"How so?" asked the stranger, after Miss Almira had disengaged herself at the elapse of a proper interval.

"Why, the Rev. Eusebius Williams has the next room. We will call him."

"But," said the stranger, "I thought the occupant of the next room was Mr. Algernon Tibbs, a gentleman from the country, who has recently sold a large number of hogs here in the city and has been ill in his room for a space by reason of a contusion on the head from a gold brick, which was, so to speak, twice thrown at his head, once figuratively as a ridiculously fine bargain which he refused to take, and again when the owner, angered, struck him with the rejected gold."

"I see," said Miss Almira archly, "that in planning for this, you have tried to study the lay of the land; but be gratified, sir, for the lucky chance which prevented a sad mistake. Mr. Tibbs and I do occupy adjoining rooms. But the one Mr. Tibbs occupies is really mine. To-day we exchanged and I will remain here for the four or five days Mr. Tibbs is to be in the city. He has a large sum of money in his possession, so we all infer. At any rate, he was afraid to sleep in this room, where there is a fire escape at the window, and took mine, where an unscalable wall prevents access. Suppose the Italian holiday had been last night and you had come then. He would then have taken you for a robber, notwithstanding that anybody could see you are a gentleman."

For the first time did Miss Almira become conscious she was not robed as one should be while receiving callers, and blushing violently, she leaped into bed, whence she bid the stranger retire for a bit until she could dress, when they would invoke the kindly offices of the Rev. Eusebius Williams.

"Your name," she called, as the stranger was about to retire.

"My name," said he impressively, "which will soon be yours, is Breckenridge Endicott."

"Mulvane," said Mr. Breckenridge Endicott to himself, noiselessly descending the stairs, "what if she had screamed before you had pulled yourself together and thought of that stunt? You didn't get old Tibb's money, but you did get—away."

Mr. Endicott tried the front door. To his apparent annoyance, there was no bolt, no knob to unlock it, and key there was none. In the parlors, he could hear the voices of boarders.

"No way there, Mulvane," said Mr. Endicott. "I'll go into the kitchen and walk out the back door. If there's anybody there, they'll think me a new boarder."

But he started violently and stood for some moments trembling for no assignable reason, as he saw in front of the range a fat German hired girl sitting in the lap of a fat Irish policeman.

"No go through Almira's room to the fire escape. But perhaps I can get out on the roof and get away somehow. She can't have dressed so soon," and he ascended the stairs to run plump into Miss Almira, who popped out of her room, resplendent in a rustling black silk.

"Oh, you impatient thing," said Miss Almira, shaking a reproving finger. "I put this on, and then I thought I ought to wear something white, and so came out to tell you not to get impatient waiting, and why I kept you so long," and back she popped.

"You are up against it, Mulvane," said Mr. Breckenridge Endicott, sitting disconsolately down upon the stairs. "Hold on, just the thing. Why, as her husband, you'll live here unsuspected and get in with old Tibbs. Why, the job will be pie. It won't be mean to her, either. When you just vanish, she'll have 'Mrs.' tacked to her name, and that'll help her. It will be lots of satisfaction. They can't call her an old maid. 'Better 'tis to have loved and lost than never to have loved at all.' I'll give her some of the boodle. She isn't bad looking. Wonder why nobody ever grabbed on to her. If I had enough to live well, I'd marry her myself and settle down."

The Rev. Eusebius Williams, with ten dollars fee in his right pantaloons pocket, and the radiant Almira, did not look happier during the wedding ceremony than did Mr. Breckenridge Endicott.

It was seldom that Mr. Endicott was absent from the side of his wife during the next few days. Occasionally pleading urgent business, he left her to go down town with Mr. Tibbs, whom he was seeking to interest in a plan to extract gold from sea water, a plan upon which Mr. Tibbs looked with some favor, for as presented by Mr. Endicott, it was one of great feasibility and promised enormous profits. In the setting forth of the method of extraction, Mr. Endicott was much aided by his wife, who overhearing him in earnest consultation with Mr. Tibbs bounded in and demanded to know what it was all about. Mr. Endicott demurred, saying it was an abstruse matter which should not burden so poetical a mind as hers. But Mr. Tibbs set it forth to her briefly. Having in her youth made much of the sciences of chemistry and physics, to the great amaze and admiration of Mr. Endicott, she launched into a most lucid explication of the practicability of the plan, leaving Mr. Tibbs more than ever inclined to venture his thousands.

"By Jove, she'll do, Mulvane. Why cut and run? Take her along. She is a splendid grafter," said Mr. Endicott to himself, as he and his wife withdrew from the presence of Mr. Tibbs. "My dear," he continued aloud, "I was overcome by respect for the way you aided me. You are indeed a jewel. I had never suspected you understood me, knew what I was, until you came in and explained that sucker trap. You are a most unexpected ally. You perceive clearly how the thing works?"

"Why, of course, Breckenridge. I have not studied science in vain, though I do not recall what part of the machine you call 'sucker trap'. Doubtless the contrivance marked 'converter,' in the drawings. Of course I understood you, right from the first, a noble, noble man, and so romantic. But Brecky, dear, why let other people share in this invention? Why not make all the money ourselves and become million, millionaires? I shall build churches and libraries and support missionaries. Why let Mr. Tibbs, who is a somewhat gross person, enjoy any of the fruits of your genius?"

Whereupon Mr. Endicott's face took on an expression of deep disappointment, disillusionment, and sorrow, until seeing his own sorrow mingled with alarm reflected on his wife's face, he presently announced that they would depart on their wedding journey by boat for Mackinac three days hence.

"I shall stop fiddle-faddling and settle the business which delays me here, at one stroke. The old simple methods are the best."

As Mr. and Mrs. Breckenridge Endicott were entering their cab to drive to the wharf, Mrs. Maxon, the landlady, came hurriedly with the scandal that Mr. Algernon Tibbs had been found in his room in the stupor of intoxication.

"Why, he might have been robbed while in that condition," said Mrs. Maxon.

"He will not be robbed while under your roof," said Mr. Endicott gallantly. "He is safe from robbing now. He will not, he cannot, I may say, be robbed now."

The sun was touching the western horizon as the steamer glided out of the river's mouth. The wind lay dead upon the water, and for a space the pair sat in the tender light of declining day indulging in the pleasures of conversation, but at length Mr. Endicott led his wife to their stateroom.

"On this auspicious day, I wish to make you a gift," and he handed her a thousand dollars in bills. "My presence is now required on the lower deck for a time. Be patient during my absence," whereupon he embraced her with an ardor he had never shown before and there was in his voice a strange ring of regret and longing such as Almira had never listened to. It thrilled her very soul and bestowing upon him a shower of passionate kisses and an embrace of the utmost affection, their parting took on almost the agony of a parting for years.

"Where the devil is that coal passer Mullanphy, I gave a job to?" said the engineer on the lower deck. "Is he aboard?"

"His dunnage is in his bunk, but nobody ain't seen him," replied one of the crew.

"Who the devil is that geezer in a Prince Albert and a plug hat that just went in back there, and what the devil is he up to?" said the engineer again, as a black-clothed figure passed toward the stern.

A few moments later, a sturdy man in a jumper and overalls, his face smeared with grime, peered cautiously around a bulkhead, and seeing nobody, stepped quickly to the side of the vessel, bearing a limp and spineless figure in a black frock and silk hat. With a dextrous movement, he cast the thing forth, and as it went flopping through the air and slapped the water, from somewhere arose the voice of Mr. Breckenridge Endicott crying, "Help! help! help!"

Mrs. Endicott, full of dole at the absence of her spouse and oppressed with a nameless disquiet, had paced the upper deck impatiently, and at this moment stood just above where her beloved went leaping to his doom.

With one wild scream, she jumped, she scrambled, she fell to the lower deck, colliding with a man leaning out looking at the sinking figure. Down, with a vain and frantic clutching at the side that only served to stay his fall so that he slipped silently into the water under the vessel's counter, went the unfortunate man.

Plump, into the yawl with the rescue crew, went Mrs. Endicott. Far astern through the dusk could be seen a black silk hat on the still water. Astern could be heard the voice of Mr. Breckenridge Endicott crying, "Quick, quick! I can swim a little, but I am almost gone!"

"Turn to the left, to the left," cried Mrs. Endicott.

"But the cries come from the right," said the coxswain.

"That's his hat to the left. I know his hat. I saw him fall. I know his voice. It's his hat and his voice."

The crew could have sworn that the cries came from the right, but to the hat they steered and the cries ceased before their arrival. They lifted the hat. Nothing beneath but eighty fathoms of water.

It was some time thereafter that a fisherman came upon a corpse floating inshore. Its face was bloated to such an extent as to prevent recognition. Its clothes were those of a steamboat roustabout. In the breastpocket was a large pocketbook bearing in gilt letters the legend, "Mr. Breckenridge Endicott."

"The present I gave him on the morning of our departure!" exclaimed Miss Almira, "now so strangely found on the dead body of the man who robbed him and probably murdered him."

Although soaked, the bills were redeemable. The fisherman was a fisherman who owned a town house on Prairie Avenue and a country house at Oconomowoc and he would take no reward. The bills amounted to nine thousand dollars. Taking her fortune, Almira retired to her former home in Ogle county, Illinois, where once more meeting Mr. Jake Long, lately made a widower, after a decent period of waiting, they became man and wife. So it ended happily for all except the person who called himself Mr. Breckenridge Endicott—though I suspect that was not his name—and for Mr. Algernon Tibbs. Lest you waste pity on Mr. Algernon Tibbs, let me say that in his youth, he was accustomed to kill little girl's cats, and that his fortune was entirely one he beat out of his brother-in-law, James Wilkinson.

WHAT BEFELL MR. MIDDLETON BECAUSE OF THE SECOND GIFT OF THE EMIR.

"THE individual whose sad taking-off I have just narrated," said the emir of the tribe of Al-Yam, "affords an excellent example of the power of good clothes. Suppose he had secreted himself under Miss Almira's bed wearing a jumper, overalls, and a mask. He would have been arrested and lodged in the penitentiary."

"But he is now dead," said Mr. Middleton.

"He had better be dead, than continuing his career of villainy and crime," quoth the emir sternly, and then passing his eyes over the person of Mr. Middleton, he remarked the somewhat threadbare and glossy garments of that excellent young man. "If you would accept a suit of raiment from me," continued the emir with a hesitation that betrayed the delicacy which was one of the most marked of the many estimable traits that made his character so admirable, "I would be overjoyed and obliged. The interests of you, my only friend in this vast land, have become to me as my own. Unfortunately I have no Frank clothes except the one suit I wear daily. But of the costumes of my native land, I have abundant store, and as we are of the same stature, I beg you will make me happy by accepting one."

Speaking some words to Mesrour in the language of Arabia, the blackamore brought in and proceeded to invest Mr. Middleton with an elegant silken habit consisting of a pair of exceedingly baggy trousers of the hue of emeralds, a round jacket whose crimson rivalled the rubies of Farther Ind, and a vest of snowy white. Double rows of small pearls ornamented the edges of the jacket, which was short and just met a copper-colored sash about the waist. After inducting him into a pair of white leggings and bronze shoes, Mesrour clapped upon his head a large white turban ornamented with a black aigret.

Mr. Middleton looked very well in his new garments and while the emir was complimenting him upon this fact and the grace of his bearing and Mr. Middleton was uttering protestations of gratitude, Mesrour busied himself, and Mr. Middleton, turning with intent to resume his wonted garb, was astonished to find it in a network of heavy twine tied with a multiplicity of knots.

"Mesrour will bring you your Frank clothes in the morning. I am very tired, and so I will bid you good night," and the yawn which now overspread the face of the accomplished prince told more than his words that the audience was ended.

Mr. Middleton looked at the bundle with its array of knots. To untie it would require a long time and the prince was repeating his yawn and his good night. Even had he not hesitated to offend the prince by demanding opportunity to resume his customary vestments and to weary him by making him wait for this operation, which promised to be a long one, he would have been without volition in the matter; for in obedience to a gesture, Mesrour grasped his arm and with great deference, but inflexible and unalterable firmness, led him through the shop and closed the street door behind him.

Mr. Middleton was greatly disconcerted at finding himself in the street arrayed in these brilliant and barbarous habiliments, but reflecting that the citizens traveling the streets at this hour would perhaps take him for some high official in one of the many fraternal orders that entertain, instruct, and edify the inhabitants of the city, he proceeded on his way somewhat reassured. As he was changing cars well toward his lodgings, at a corner where a large public hall reared its façade, he heard himself accosted, and turning, beheld a portly person wearing a gilt paper crown, a long robe of purple velvet bordered with rabbit's fur spotted with black, and bearing in his hand a bung-starter, which, covered with gilt paper, made a very creditable counterfeit of a royal scepter.

"Come here once," said this personage.

With great affableness expressing a willingness to come twice, if it were desired, Mr. Middleton accompanied the personage, as with an air of brooding mystery, the latter led him down the street twenty feet from where they had first stood.

"Was you going to the masquerade?"

"Yes," said Mr. Middleton, divining from the presence of the personage and two other masquers whom he now beheld entering the hall, that a masquerade was in progress.

"What'll you take to stay away?"

"Why?"

"You'll take the prize."

"What is the prize and why should the possibility of winning it deter me?"

"The prize is five dollars. It's this way. I am a saloonkeeper. Gustaf Kleiner and I are in love with the same girl. She is in love with all both of us. She don't know what to say. She can't marry all both, so she says she'll marry the one what gits the prize at the masquerade. If you git the prize, don't either of us git the girl already. I'll give you twenty dollars to stay away."

"But what of Gustaf Kleiner? Have you paid him?"

"He is going to be a devil. I hired two Irishmans for five dollars to meet him up the street, cut off his tail, break his horns, and put whitewash on his red suit. He is all right. I'll make it thirty dollars and a ticket of the raffle for my watch to-morrow."

"Done," said Mr. Middleton, and he proceeded to draw up a contract binding him to stay away from the masquerade for a consideration of thirty dollars.

It was not the least remarkable part of his adventure that he did not meet Gustaf Kleiner in his damaged suit and for a consideration of fifty dollars, lend him the magnificent Oriental costume. He did not see Gustaf Kleiner at all, nor did he win the watch in the raffle and the chronicler hopes that the setting down of these facts will not cause the readers to doubt his veracity, for he is aware that usually these things are ordered differently.

Having kept the Oriental costume for several days and seeing no prospect of ever wearing it, and his small closet having become crowded by the presence of a new twenty-dollar suit which he purchased with part of his gains, he presented it to the young lady in Englewood previously mentioned, who reduced the ruby red jacket to a beautiful bolero jacket, made a table throw of the sash, and after much hesitation seized the exceedingly baggy trousers—which were made with but one seam—and ripping them up, did, with a certain degree of confusion, fashion them into two lovely shirt waists. But she did not wear them in the presence of Mr. Middleton and did not even mention them to him. Nor did Mr. Middleton allude to any of these transactions when on the appointed day and hour he again sat in the presence of the urbane prince of the tribe of Al-Yam. Handing him a bowl of delicately flavored sherbet, Achmed began to narrate The Adventure of William Hicks.

THE ADVENTURE OF WILLIAM HICKS.

YOUNG WILLIAM HICKS was a native of the village of Bensonville, in the southern part of Illinois. Having, at the age of twenty, graduated at the head of a class of six in the village school, his father thought to reward him for his diligence in study by a short trip to the city of Chicago, which metropolis William had never beheld. Addressing him in a discourse which, while not long, abounded in valuable advice, Mr. Hicks presented his son with a sum of money sufficient for a stay of a week, provided it were not expended imprudently.

One evening, William was walking along Wabash Avenue, feeling somewhat lonely as he soberly reflected that not one in all that vast multitude cared anything about him, when he heard himself accosted in a most cheery manner, and looking up, beheld a beautiful lady smiling at him. It was plain that she belonged to the upper classes. A hat of very large proportions, ornamented with a great ostrich plume, shaded a head of lovely yellow hair. She was clothed all in rustling purple silk and sparkled with jewelry. Her cheeks and lips glowed with a carmine quite unknown among the fair but pale damosels of Bensonville, which is situated in a low alluvial location, surrounded by flat plains, the whole being somewhat damp and malarial. William had never imagined eyes so wide open and glistening.

"My name is Willy, to be sure. But you have the advantage of me, for ashamed as I am to say it, I cannot quite recall you. You are not the lady who came to Bensonville and stayed at the Campbellite minister's?"

"Oh, how are all the dear folks in Bensonville? But, say, Will, don't you want to come along with me awhile and talk it all over?"

"I should be honored to do so, if you will lead the way. I confess I am lonely to-night, and I always enjoy talking over old times."

At this juncture, a sudden look of alarm spread over the lady's beauteous face and a lumbering minion of the law stepped before her.

"Up to your old tricks, eh?" he growled. "Didn't I tell you that the next time I caught you tackling a man, I'd run you in? Run you in it is. Come on, now."

"Oh, oh," panted the lady, and great tears welled into her adorable eyes. At that moment, there was a crash in the street, as a poor Italian exile had his push cart overturned by the sudden and unexpected backing of a cab. The policeman turned to look and, like a frightened gazelle, the lady bounded away, closely followed by young William.

"Is there nothing I can do? Cannot I complain to the judge for you, or address a communication to some paper describing and condemning this conduct?"

"Is he coming? Is he coming?" asked the lady, piteously.

"No. But if he were, I would strike him, big as he is. Cannot a former visitor in Bensonville greet one of its citizens without interference from the police?"

Hereupon the lady, who seemed to be giving little heed to what William was saying, beyond the information that the policeman was not in pursuit, gave a gay little laugh of relief, which caused William's eyes to light in pitying sympathy.

"Now that we are away from him, what do you say to a friendly game of cards somewhere, to pass away the evening, which hangs heavy on my hands and doubtless does on yours?"

"I have never played cards," said William, "for while there is nothing intrinsically wrong in them, they are the vehicle of much that is injurious, and at the very least, they cause one to fritter away valuable time in profitless amusement."

"Oh, la! you are wrong there," said the lady, with a little silvery laugh. "They are not a profitless amusement. Why, a man has to keep his brains in good trim when he plays cards, and whist is just as good a mental exercise as geometry and algebra, or any other study where the mind is engaged upon various problems. You see I stand up for cards, for I teach whist myself and I assure you that many of the leading ladies of this city spend their time in little else than whist, which they would not do if cards were what you say. Before you pass your opinion, why not let me show you some of the fine points, and then you will have something to base your judgment upon."

William, quite impressed by the elegance and social standing of the lady, as well as influenced by her beauty, despite her evident seniority of ten or fifteen years, assented, and the lady continued:

"I would invite you to my own apartments, but they are so far away, and as we are now in front of the Hotel Dieppe, let us go up and engage a room for a few hours and I will teach you a few little interesting tricks with which you can amuse the people of Bensonville, and even obtain some profit, if you wish to. What do you say?"

William averring that he would be pleased to receive the proffered instruction, she led the way up a flight of stairs and paused in the doorway of the hotel office, for the Hotel Dieppe was a hostelry of no great pretentions and occupied the upper stories of a building, the lower floors of which were devoted to a furniture emporium. Behind the counter stood a low-browed clerk with a large diamond in his shirt front, who scrutinized them keenly.

"You get the room," said the lady, coyly. "I'm bashful and don't like to go in there where are all those smoking men. You may take it in my name if you wish,—Madeleine Montmorency."

"Number 15," said the clerk, and in a space William found himself in a dark room, alone with the lady, and heard the door close behind them and the key turn in the lock.

"We are locked in!" exclaimed Miss Montmorency.

"What's that?" said a deep voice in the darkness.

Miss Montmorency screamed, and screamed again as William turned on the light and they beheld a man lying in bed!

William was stepping hastily to her side to shield her vision from this improper spectacle, when he paused as if frozen to the floor. The man was now sitting up in bed and he had a red flannel night gown, one eye, AND TWO NOSES!

"What the devil are you doing here?" exclaimed the monster in the red flannel nightgown.

"That I will gladly tell you, for I would not have you believe that we wantonly intruded upon your slumbers." And thereupon William related that he was a citizen of Bensonville who had met a former visitor there and they had come here to talk over mutual acquaintances and improve their minds by discreet discourse. "But, sir," he said, in concluding, "pardon my natural curiosity concerning yourself. Who are you and why are you?"

"If I had the printed copies of my life here, I would gladly sell you one, but I left them all behind. My name is Walker Sheldrup. I am registered from Springfield, Mass., but I am from Dubuque, Iowa. I was born in Sedalia, Mo., where my father was a prominent citizen. It was he who led the company of men who, with five ox teams, hauled the courthouse away from Georgetown and laid the foundations of Sedalia's greatness. Had he lived, Sedalia would not have tried in vain to swipe the capital from Jefferson City. As a youth I was distinguished—but I'll cut all that out. Your presence here and the door being locked behind you only too surely warns me that we have no time to lose. They have taken you for the snake-eating lady and the rubber-skinned boy, who ran away when I did and who were to meet me here in Chicago. If you will turn your heads away so I can dress, I will continue. You have heard of prenatal influences. Shortly before I was born, my mother made nine pumpkin pies and set them to cool on a stone wall beneath the shade of a large elm. As luck would have it, a menagerie passed by and an elephant grabbed those pies one after another and ate them. The sight of that enormous pachyderm gobbling my mother's cherished handiwork, completely upset her. I was born with two noses like the two tusks of the beast. At the same time, like the trunk, they are movable. My two noses are as mobile and useful as two fingers and if you have a quarter with you, I will gladly perform some curious feats. My noses being so near together, ordinarily, I join them with flesh-colored wax. I then seem to have but one nose, although a very large one. I thus escape the annoying attention of the multitude, which is very disagreeable to a proud man of good family, like me. Young man, do you ever drink? In Dubuque, they got me drunk so I didn't know what I was about and I signed a contract with a dime museum company for twenty-five dollars a week. Take warning from my fate. Never drink, never drink."

"I can well imagine your sufferings at being a spectacle for a ribald crowd," said William. "To a man of refined sensibilities, it must be excruciating, and it was an outrage to entrap you into such a contract."

"I ought to have had seventy-five and could have got fifty. So I ran away. Well, now, how are we going to get out of here? Can you climb over the transom, young man?"

As he said these words, the door flew open and in rushed some villainous looking men, who gagged, handcuffed, and shackled Miss Montmorency, William, and the two-nosed man.

"We have the legal right to do this," said the leader, displaying the badge of the Jinkins private detective agency. "Advices from Dubuque set us at work. We early located Sheldrup at this hotel, and when the clerk saw the rubber-skinned boy and the snake-eating lady come in, he suspicioned who they was at once and by a great stroke, put 'em in with old two-nose. Do you think we are going to put you through for breach of contract and for swiping that money out of the till on the claim it was due you on salary? Nit. Cost too much, take too much time, and you git sent to jail instead of being back in the museum helping draw crowds. We are in for saving time and trouble for you, us, and your employer. To-night you ride out of here for Dubuque, covered up with hay, in the corner of the car carrying the new trick horse for the museum. Save your fare and all complications. Now, boys, we want to work this on the quiet, so we will just leave 'em all here until the streets are deserted and there won't be anybody around to notice us gitting 'em into the hack."

"Hadn't one of us better stay?" asked a subordinate.

"How can people gagged, their ankles shackled, their hands handcuffed behind 'em, git out? Why, I'll just leave the handcuff keys here on the table and tantalize 'em."

Tears welled in the soft, beauteous orbs of Miss Montmorency and William's eyes spoke keen distress, but Mr. Sheldrup's eyes gleamed triumphantly above the cloth tied about the lower part of his face. Hardly had the steps of the detectives died away on the stair, when a little click was heard behind Miss Montmorency and her handcuffs fell to the floor. There stood Mr. Sheldrup, politely bowing, with the key held between his two noses. She seized it and in a twinkling, the bonds of all had been removed and, forcing the door, they started away. At the street entrance stood the policeman who had insulted Miss Montmorency!

"Oh, he's waiting for me, and I'll get six months. He knew where I'd go. I haven't any money," and tears not only filled the wondrous optics of poor Miss Montmorency, but flowed down her cheeks.

"Six months, your grandmother. I'll not go back on you. Young man, follow me into the office and when I am fairly in front of the clerk, give me a shove," and the two-nosed man, with a grip in each hand, walked up to the clerk and began to rebuke him for his ungentlemanly and unprincipled conduct.

"You white-livered son of a sea-cook, you double-dyed, concentrated essence of a skunk," and at that moment young William pushed him and the two-nosed gentleman lurched forward, and bending his head to avoid contact with the clerk's face, it rested against the latter's bosom for a moment. Departing immediately, at the foot of the stairs the two-nosed gentleman said to the policeman:

"Officer, please let this lady pass. For various reasons, I desire it enough to spare this stud, which will look well upon the best policeman on the force."

"All right," said the policeman. "Go along for all of me, Bet Higgins," and he courteously accepted the diamond.

"My stage name," said Miss Montmorency, in answer to an inquiring look from William. "The name I sign to articles in the Sunday papers."

"Now of course they are watching all the depots," said the two-nosed gentleman. "Before they located me here they did that, and as they have also been looking for the snake-eating lady and the rubber-skinned boy, our late captors have not had time to notify them that we have been captured. It is useless to try to escape that way, then; it is too far to walk out, or go by street car, and as it is a fair, moonlight night with a soft breeze, I am for getting a boat and sailing out."

After some search, they found a small sail boat. Miss Montmorency had decided to flee from the wicked city with the two-nosed gentleman. She had heard such delightful reports of Michigan. The owner of the boat not being there and there being no probability that they would ever return it, the two-nosed gentleman wrote a check on a Dubuque bank for one hundred and seventy-five dollars, and Miss Montmorency an order on the school board for a like amount, and these they pinned up where the boatman could find them.

"It will be quite like a fairy tale when the good boatman comes in the morning and finds this large sum left him by those to whom his little craft has been of such inestimable service," said William, and then for fear the boatman might not find the check and the order, in two other places he pinned up cards giving the whereabouts of the remuneration for the boat and some statement concerning the circumstances of its requisition. On the back of one of the cards had been penciled his name and city address, and though he had erased the black of this inscription, the impression yet remained distinctly legible. This erasure was not due to any desire to conceal his identity or lodgings, but because he had thought at first that he could not get all the information on one side of the card. Having seen his friends go slipping out on the deep, he turned pensively homeward, somewhat heavy of heart, for when one faces perils with another, fast friendships are quickly welded.

In the morning, young William was arrested and lodged in jail and a corrupt and venal judge laughed with contempt at his plea. After three long days in jail, came Mr. Hicks, senior, who compounded with the boat owner for two hundred and fifty dollars, the boat being, as the owner swore, of Spanish cedar with nickel-plated trimmings.

"That is always the way when a person of good heart befriends another," said Mr. Middleton.

"Alas, too often," said the emir of the tribe of Al-Yam. "But I am pleased to say that when once across the lake, the two-nosed gentleman married Miss Montmorency, who whatever she might be, did not lack certainly womanly qualities and had been the sport of an unkind world. Having something to live for, the two-nosed gentleman signed with a Detroit dime museum company at seventy-five dollars a week. His two noses were not the most remarkable thing about him, for in course of time hearing of young William's misadventure, he sent him a sum equivalent to all the episode had cost him, together with a handsome diamond stud, which he had with great deftness and cleverness taken from the officious policeman, as he visited the dime museum with two ladies while spending his vacation in Detroit. And this beautiful ornament William delighted to wear, not merely because of its intrinsic worth, which was considerable, but through regard for its thoughtful and considerate donor."

"The two-nosed man did truly show himself a man of gratitude, and I am glad to hear of such an instance. Yet from what you said of him in the beginning of the tale, I should not have expected it of him. How often is one deceived by appearances and how hard it is to trust to them."

"Even the wisest is unable to distinguish an enemy wearing the guise of a friend, but we may bring to our assistance the aid of forces more powerful than our poor little human intelligence. Let me present you with a talisman which will ever warn you when any one plots against you."

"How?"

"How? You must wait until some one plots against you and the talisman will answer that question. Its ways of warning will be as manifold as the plots villains may conceive. Here is the talisman, an Egyptian scarabæus of pure gold. So cunningly fashioned is it that not nature itself made ever a bug more perfect in the outward seeming."

WHAT BEFELL MR. MIDDLETON BECAUSE OF THE THIRD GIFT OF THE EMIR.

PUTTING the scarabæus in his left trousers pocket, Mr. Middleton departed, and as he went about his affairs during the next several days, he ceased to think of the talisman, but on the fourth day his attention was recalled to it in a way that indeed seemed to prove that it was a charm possessed of the powers the emir of the tribe of Al-Yam had attributed to it. He was faring northward in a street car at eleven of the morning, diverting himself with the study of the passengers sitting opposite, when he became aware that the scarabæus in his left trousers pocket was slowly traveling up his leg. Had the talisman been other than the heavy object it was, he would not have noticed it, but it was of too considerable weight to travel over his person without making its progress felt. Deterred by none of the superstitious tremors which the unaccountable peregrinations of the gold beetle would have excited in one less intrepid, he quickly thrust his hand into his pocket to close it over another hand already there, a hand which beyond a first little start to escape, lay passive and unresisting, a hand soft and delicate, yet well-muscled withal, long-fingered and finely formed. At the same time, a well-modulated voice at his side exclaimed:

"Why, I did not recognize you at first. I was not looking when you came and you evidently did not notice me."

"No, I did not," said Mr. Middleton, composedly, still retaining his grasp upon the hand in his pocket. "I cannot see that you have changed any," he continued, scrutinizing the young woman at his side, for she was young and, moreover, of a very pleasing presence, and he did not altogether rebel against the circumstances that allowed him to fondle the hand of one so comely. The day, which had begun with a slight chill, had turned off warm and she had removed her cloak, which, lying across her own lap and partially across Mr. Middleton's, had been the blind behind which she had introduced her hand into the pocket where reposed the fateful talisman.

The persons in the car seemed to take an interest in this sudden recognition on the part of a pair who had been riding side by side for so long, oblivious of each other's identity. Moreover, the young woman was tastefully gowned and of a very smart appearance, while Mr. Middleton's new suit became him and fitted him nicely and altogether they were a couple nearly any one would find pleasure in looking upon. A slight movement to withdraw the hand lying within his own, caused Mr. Middleton's grasp to tighten and almost simultaneously, the young woman at his side leaned forward and with a look in which sorrow and pain were mingled, said in a lowered voice:

"Oh, I have such a dreadful thing to tell you about our friend Amy. I hate to tell you, but as I wish to bespeak your kind offices, I must do so. I am going to ask you to be the agent of a restitution. She has, oh, she has become a kleptomaniac. With every luxury, with her fine home on the Lake Shore Drive, with all her father's wealth, with no want money can gratify, she takes things. In her circumstances it is out of the question to call it stealing. It is a mania, a form of insanity. When she is doing it, she seems to be in the grasp of some other mind, to be another person, and her actions are involuntary, unconscious. Then she seems to come to herself, when her agony is dreadful to behold."

The young woman's voice broke a little here, she paused a moment to resume control of herself, and perceiving her eyes swimming with tears and her lips quivering with unhappiness, Mr. Middleton was penetrated with pity and pressed most tenderly and sympathetically the delicate hand of which he was temporarily custodian.

"She took things in stores, trumpery, cheap things. She took magazines and penny papers from news stands. But oh, she descended to the dreadful depths of—oh, I can hardly tell it—she was detected in trying to pick a man's pocket. It is here that I wish to employ you as an agent of restitution, or rather retribution, I should say. Will you please take this ring off my left hand and take it to the man she tried to rob? I cannot use the fingers of my right hand owing to temporary incapacitation," and she held out to Mr. Middleton her left hand, upon the third finger of which gleamed a splendid ring of diamonds and emeralds. Mr. Middleton possessed himself of this second hand, but paused, and regarding the sweet face turned up to his so beseechingly, so piteously, said:

"But that would be compounding a felony. And how do you know the man will not have her arrested anyway?"

"The man is a gentleman and having heard her story, will not think of such a thing. You are to ask him to accept the ring not as a price for immunity from arrest, but as a punishment, a retribution to Amy. The loss of the ring, which she has commissioned me to get to this gentleman in some manner, will be a lesson she is only too anxious to give herself, a forcible reminder, as it were. Let me beg of you to undertake this commission."

All the while, Mr. Middleton was retaining hold of both the hands of the sorrowful young woman. Had they been other than the soft and shapely hands they were, had they been hard and gnarled and large, long before would he, melted by compassion at the young woman's tale, have released her. But her very charms had been her undoing and because of her perfect hands, this tale has grown long. That he might have excuse in the eyes of the other passengers for holding the young woman's hand, Mr. Middleton removed the ring as he had been bidden, planning to return it shortly. As he removed the ring, he released the hand in his pocket and his plan was frustrated by the young woman starting up with the exclamation that she had passed her corner, and springing from the car. She was so far in advance of him, when he succeeded in getting off the car and was walking so rapidly, that he could not overtake her except by running, and he was averse to attracting the attention that this would occasion. So he determined to shadow her and ascertaining her residence, find some means of restoring the ring without the knowledge of her friends, as he had no desire to do anything which might cause them to learn of her unfortunate infirmity, especially, as this last experience might have worked a cure. She did indeed enter a stately mansion of the Lake Shore Drive—but by the back door.

Pondering upon this episode, Mr. Middleton went to an acquaintance who kept a large loan bank on Madison Street, who, after discovering that he had no desire to pawn the ring, appraised it at seven hundred dollars.

On the following evening, Mr. Middleton was replacing his new suit by his old, as was his custom when he intended to remain in his room of an evening. This example cannot be too highly commended to all young men. The amount which would be saved in this nation were all to economize in this way, would be sufficient to buy beer for all the Teutonic citizens of the large state of Illinois. As Mr. Middleton was changing his clothes, the scarabæus dropped from his pocket and as he picked it up, a collar button fell from his neckband, and scrambling for it as it rolled toward the unexplored regions under his bed, he tripped and sprawled at full length, his nose coming in sharp contact with an evening paper lying on the floor. He was about to rise from his recumbent position, when his eyes, glancing along his nose to discover if it had sustained any injury, observed that said member rested upon a notice which read:

> "Lost, a diamond and emerald ring. $800 will be paid for its return and no questions asked. David O. Crecelius."

The address was that of the house on the Lake Shore Drive which the kleptomaniac had entered! Once more did the scarabæus seem to be exerting its influence. But for the talisman, he would never have seen the notice, and a little shiver ran through him as he thought of this. Immediately he reclothed himself in his new suit.

"There is time for me to think out a course of action between here and my destination," said he. "The walking so conducive to reflection can be much better employed in taking me toward the Lake Shore Drive, than in uselessly pacing my room, and I'll be there when I get through."

As he traveled eastward, he engaged in a series of ratiocinative processes and the result of the deductive and inductive reasoning which he applied to the case in hand, was as follows:

The kleptomaniac could hardly be a daughter of the house. She would have entered by the front door. If she were the daughter of the house, she would not have had the ring advertised for, counting herself fortunate to get out of the difficulty so cheaply. However, if her parents had noted the absence of the ring, she might have said it was lost and so they advertised, but nothing could have been further from her wishes, for there would be the great danger that the outcome of the advertisement would be a complete exposure. She could easily prevent her parents noticing the ring was gone, at least making satisfactory explanations for not wearing it. With her wealth, she could have it duplicated inside of a few days and her friends never know the original was lost. As this is what the daughter of the house in all probability would have done, the kleptomaniac could hardly have been the daughter of the house. He suspected that she was a lady's maid, who, wearing her mistress's jewelry, had purchased her way out of one difficulty at the risk of getting into another. The advertisement would seem to indicate that she was trusted. The disappearance of the ring was apparently not connected with her. The matter was very simple. He would hand over the ring and take the eight hundred dollars and need say nothing that would implicate the young woman, be she daughter of the house and kleptomaniac, or serving-maid and common thief. But one thing puzzled him. Why was the reward greater than the value of the ring?

Eight hundred dollars. The young lady in Englewood was getting nearer.

A bitter east wind was blowing as he walked up to the entrance of the mansion of Mr. David Crecelius. Behind him the street lay all deserted and the melancholy voice of the waves filled the air. Nowhere could he see a light about the house and he was oppressed by a feeling of undefinable apprehension as he pressed the bell. A considerable interval elapsing without any one appearing and a second and a third ringing failing to elicit any response from within the silent pile, he was about to depart, feeling greatly relieved that it was not necessary to hold parley with any one within the gloomy and forbidding edifice, when he heard a sudden light thud at his feet and discovered that the scarabæus had dropped through a hole in his trousers' pocket which had at that moment reached a size large enough to allow it to escape. After a hurried search, he had possessed himself of the talisman and was about to depart, when the door swung open before him and a venerable white-haired man stood in a dim green glow. Boldly did Mr. Middleton enter, for had not the talisman delayed him until the venerable man opened the door?

"Come in, sir, come in," said the venerable man, whom Mr. Middleton saw was none other than David O. Crecelius, the capitalist, whose portraits he had seen again and again in the Sunday papers and the weekly papers of a moral and entertaining nature, accompanying accounts of his life and achievements, with exhortations to the youth of the land to imitate them, advice which Mr. Middleton then and there resolved to follow, reflecting upon the impeccable sources from which it emanated.

"All the servants seem to be gone. My family is abroad and the household force has been cut down, and I have given everybody leave to go out to-night, all but one maid, and she seems to have gone, too," said Mr. Crecelius, leading Mr. Middleton into a spacious salon and seating him near where great portières of a funereal purple moved uneasily in the superheated atmosphere of the house. At that moment, a voice from the hallway, a voice he had surely heard before, said:

"Did some one ring? I am very sorry, but it was impossible for me to come," and Mr. Middleton was aware that some one was looking hard at the back of his head.

"Yes. I let them in. It's no matter. Run away now."

When Mr. Middleton had finished explaining the reason for his call and had fished up the ring, Mr. Crecelius did not, as he had expected he would, arise and make out a check for $800.

"This ring," said that gentleman after a little pause, "have you it with you?"

Mr. Middleton glanced at the hollow of his left hand. He had fished up the scarabæus instead of the ring. But his left thumb soon showed him the ring was safe in his vest pocket. The delay and caution of Mr. Crecelius, and above all, the prevention of the immediate delivery of the ring caused by the scarabæus coming up in its stead caused Mr. Middleton to delay.

"It can be produced," said he.

"How did you get it?"

"It came into my possession innocently enough so far as I was concerned. As to the person from whom I received it, that is a different matter, but though I made no promises, I feel I am in honor bound not to disclose that person's identity."

As he uttered these words, Mr. Middleton saw the portière at his side rustle slightly. It was not the swaying caused by the currents of overheated air.

"I will give you two hundred dollars more to tell me who gave you or sold you the ring."

"I cannot do that."

"Very well. I'll only give you four hundred dollars reward."

"The ring is worth more than that."

"If you retain it, or sell it, you become a thief."

"You have advertised eight hundred dollars reward and no questions asked. I may have found it. Knowing of your loss through reading your advertisement, I may have gone to great trouble to recover it. At any rate, I have it. I deliver it. Your advertisement is in effect a contract which I can call upon you to carry out. The ring is not mine, but for my services in getting it, I am entitled to the eight hundred dollars you agree to give. You cannot give less."

"Do you think it right to take advantage of my necessity in this way? You ought to accept less. The ring is not worth over seven hundred dollars. For returning it, three hundred dollars ought to be enough. It is wrong to drive a hard bargain by taking advantage of my necessity."

"You have built your fortune on such principles. You have engineered countless schemes and your dollars came from the straits you reduced others to."

"But do you think it right? What I may have done, does not justify you. I venture to say you and other young chaps have sat with heels cocked up and pipes in mouth and discussed me and called me a villain for doing what you are trying to do with me."

"I have indeed. But that was in the past and I have changed my views materially. At present, I have the exclusive possession of the ability to secure something you very much want. You offered eight hundred dollars. Intrinsically, the ring is not worth it, but for certain reasons, possession of the ring is worth eight hundred dollars."

"Possession of the ring! Certain reasons!" said Mr. Crecelius, springing to his feet and pacing up and down the room angrily. As Mr. Middleton was cudgelling his brains to find some reason for this outburst of anger, he became cognizant of a small piece of folded paper lying near his feet. He was about to pick it up and hand it to the financier, when he was stayed by the reflection that it might have dropped from his own pocket and examining it, read:

> "It's his wife's ring. I wore it along with some of her other things. Ten years ago, he gave it to another woman, and his wife found it out and he had to buy it back. He is afraid his wife will think he gave the ring away a second time. That is why I dared give it to you. Make him give you a thousand.
>
> "The One You Didn't Give Away."

Mr. Middleton put the note in his pocket, and the eminent capitalist having ceased pacing and standing gazing at him, he remarked:

"Certain reasons, such as preventing an altercation with your wife over her suspicions that you had not lost the ring, but had disposed of it as on a former occasion ten years since."

"Young man, you cannot blackmail me. My wife knows all about that. The knowledge of that occurrence is worthless as a piece of blackmail."

"As blackmail, yes; but not worthless as an indication of the extent you desire to regain possession of the ring. Your wife knows of your former escapade and that is gone and past. But the present disappearance of the ring will cause her to think you have repeated the escapade. This knowledge of certain conditions causes me to see that my services in securing and delivering the ring are worth one thousand dollars. Upon the payment of that sum, cash, I hand you the ring."

The distinguished money-king gave Mr. Middleton a very black look and then left the room to return almost immediately with a thousand dollars in bills, which Mr. Middleton counted, placed in his vest pocket, and forthwith delivered the ring. As he did so, yielding to the pride with which the successful outcome of his tilt with the great capitalist inflamed him, he remarked with a condescension which the suavity of his tones could not conceal:

"Had you, sir, employed in this affair the perspicacity you have displayed on so many notable occasions, it would have occurred to you that this ring, being of a common pattern, could be duplicated for seven hundred dollars and so you be saved both money and worry."

A look of admiration overspread the face of the eminent manipulator, and grasping Mr. Middleton's hand with great fervor, he exclaimed:

"A man after my own heart. I am always ready to acknowledge a defeat. You have good stuff in you. I must know you better. You must stay and have a glass of champagne with me. I will get it myself," and he hurried out of the room.

In the state of Wisconsin, from which Mr. Middleton hailed, there is a great deal of the alcoholic beverage, beer, but such champagne as is to be found there is all due to importation, since it is not native to the soil, but is brought in at great expense from France, La Belle France, and New Jersey, La Belle New Jersey. Mr. Middleton had seen, smelled, and tasted beer, but champagne was unknown to him save by hearsay, and his improper curiosity and his readiness to succumb to temptation caused him to linger in the salon of Mr. Crecelius, thereby nearly accomplishing his ruin. Suddenly there was a patter of light steps across the floor, a hand fell lightly on his shoulder and a voice lightly on his ear.

"You made him raving mad when you said what you did. He telephoned the police. Now he has gone for the wine and will try to hold you until they come."

"But he cannot arrest me. I have done nothing," said Mr. Middleton, his heart going pit-a-pat, in spite of the boldness of his words.

"He can make all sorts of trouble for you. Even if you did come out all right in the end, think of the trouble. Come, come quick!"

A soft hand had grasped one of his and he was up and away, following his fair guide up stairs, through the house, and down into the kitchen.

"I have recovered my wits a bit," said Mr. Middleton. "He is so angry that he has no thought but immediate vengeance, and so accordingly telephones the police, and if they were to catch me here, it certainly would be bad. But to-morrow he will be in a mood to appreciate the good sense of the letter I shall send him, calling his attention to the fact that if he arrests me, in the trial there must come out the reason why I demanded one thousand dollars, the story of his domestic indiscretion, and so he will not think of pursuing the matter further."

"It was very kind and very noble of you not to expose me," said the young woman in a voice in which gratitude and sadness were mingled; "and all the admiration and gratitude a woman can feel under such circumstances, I feel toward you. To you I owe my continued good name and even my very freedom. I know that marriage with such as you, is not for such as me. I am going to ask you to give to her who would have all, but expects and deserves nothing, the consolation of a kiss. Whatever happy maiden may be so fortunate as to receive your love, I shall have treasured in memory the golden remembrance that once my preserver bestowed on me the symbol of love."

Mr. Middleton looked down at the girl, supplicating for the favor her sex is wont to deny, and he said to himself that seldom had he seen a more flower-like face. Her lovely lips were already puckered in a rosy pout, her hands raised ready to rest on his shoulders as he should encircle her with his arms, when he noted with a start that her eyes, snapping, alert, and eager, were bent not upon his face, but upon his upper left hand vest pocket, where bulged the one thousand dollars in bills.

"I am more than honored and I shall be ravished with delight to comply. But here, where we stand, we are exposed to view from three sides. If Mr. Crecelius were to look in and see you being kissed by me, whom he so dislikes, in what a bad plight you would be. Not even for the exquisite pleasure of kissing you would I subject you to such a danger. But in the shadow by the outer door, we would not be seen."

As he said these words, Mr. Middleton placed the money in his inside vest pocket, buttoned his vest, buttoned his inner coat, and buttoned his overcoat, moving toward the outer door as he did so, the young woman following him more and more slowly, the light in her eyes dying with each successive buttoning. In fact, she did not enter into the shadow at all, and Mr. Middleton stepped back a bit when he threw his arms about her and pressed her to his bosom. Perfunctorily and coldly did she yield to his embrace, but whatever ardor was lacking on her part, was compensated for by Mr. Middleton, who clasped her with exceeding tightness and showered kisses upon her pouting lips until she pushed him from her, exclaiming with annoyance:

"You've kissed me quite enough, you great big softy."

Mr. Middleton said nothing of these transactions when on the ensuing evening he sat in the presence of the young lady of Englewood, nor did he, when on the evening thereafter he once more sat in the presence of the urbane prince of the tribe of Al-Yam. Having handed him a bowl of delicately flavored sherbet, Achmed began to narrate The Adventure of Nora Sullivan and the Student of Heredity.

THE ADVENTURE OF NORAH SULLIVAN AND THE STUDENT OF HEREDITY.

IT WAS the time of full moon. As the orb of day dropped its red, huge disk below the western horizon, over the opposite side of the world, the moon, even more huge and scarcely less red, rose to irradiate with its mild beams the scenes which the shadows of darkness had not yet touched. Miss Nora Sullivan, a teacher in the public schools of the metropolis, sat upon the front porch of the paternal residence enjoying the loveliness of the vernal prospect and the balm of the air, for it was in the flowery month of June. Although the residence of Timothy Sullivan was well within the limits of the municipality of Chicago, one visiting at that hospitable abode might imagine himself in the country. From no part of the enclosure could you, during the leafy season, see another human habitation. A quarter of a mile down the road to the east, the electric cars for Calumet could be seen flitting by, but except at the intervals of their passing, there was seldom anything to suggest that the location was part of a great city. A quarter of a mile to the west, on the edge of a marsh—a situation well suited to such culture—lived a person engaged in the raising of African geese. As it is probable that you may never have heard of African geese, I will tell you that they are the largest of their tribe and that specimens of them often weigh as high as seventy pounds.

The person engaged in the culture of African geese was Wilhelm Klingenspiel, a man of German ancestry, but born in this country. Miss Sullivan had often heard of him, she had even partaken of the left leg of an African goose, which leg he had given Mr. Sullivan for the Sunday dinner, but she had never seen him. As Wilhelm Klingenspiel was young and single and as no other man of any description lived in the vicinity, it is not strange that Nora, who was also young and single, should sometimes fall to thinking of Mr. Klingenspiel and wonder what manner of man he was.

On this evening so attuned to romantic reveries, when the flowers, the birds, and all nature spoke of love, more than ever did Nora Sullivan's thoughts turn toward the large grove of trees to the westward in the midst of which Wilhelm Klingenspiel had his home and carried on his pleasant and harmless vocation of raising African geese. The evening song of the geese, tempered and sweetened by distance, came to her, accompanied by the most extraordinary booming and racketing of frogs which is to be heard outside of the tropical zone; for not only did Klingenspiel raise the largest geese on this terraqueous globe, but having, as a means of cheapening the cost of their production, devoted himself to the increasing of their natural food, by principles well known to all breeders he had developed a breed of frogs as monstrous among their kind as African geese are among theirs. By these huge batrachians was an extensive marsh inhabited, and battening upon the succulent nutriment thus afforded, the African geese gained a size and flavor which was rapidly making the fortune of Wilhelm Klingenspiel.

Nora had often meditated upon plans for making the acquaintance of Wilhelm, but it was plain that he was either very bashful or so immersed in his pursuits as to be indifferent to the charms of woman, for he had never made an attempt to see Nora in all the six months she had been his neighbor, and she was well worth seeing.

Accordingly, she decided that if she did not wish to indefinitely postpone making the acquaintance of the poulterer, she must take the initiative. Timothy Sullivan was a market gardener. Klingenspiel was not the only man in the neighborhood who grew big things. Mr. Sullivan was experimenting upon some cabbages of unusual size. He had started them in a hothouse during the winter. Later transferred to the garden, they had attained an amplitude such as few if any cabbages had ever attained before. In the pleasant light of the moon, even now was he engaged with the cabbages, pouring something upon them from a watering pot. As she watched her father, it occurred to Nora that she could find no more suitable excuse for visiting Mr. Klingenspiel than in carrying him some present in return for the goose's left leg he had presented her family for a Sunday dinner, and that there was no more appropriate present than one of the great cabbages.

No sooner had her father gone in than, selecting the largest cabbage, she started off with it, putting it in a small push-cart, as it was so large as to be too heavy and inconvenient to carry. It was somewhat late to call, but the evening was so delightful that Wilhelm Klingenspiel could hardly have gone to bed. Proceeding on her way, as the road passed into the swampy land of Klingenspiel's domain, her attention was engaged by the fact that a most singular commotion was taking place among the giant batrachians at some remote place south of the road. Their ordinary calls had increased both in volume and frequency, and at intervals she heard the sound of crashing in the brake and brush, as if some objects of unheard of size were falling into the marsh. Looking in the direction whence the sounds came, she saw indistinct and vague against the night sky, an enormous rounded thing rise in the air and descend, whereupon was borne to her another of the strange crashings. These inexplicable sounds and the inexplicable sight would have frightened Miss Sullivan had she not the resources with which modern science fortifies the mind against credulity and superstition. The round object, she told herself, was some sudden puff of smoke on a railway track far beyond; the crashing was the shunting of cars, which things, coming coincidentally with a battle of the frogs, to an ignorant mind would appear to be a phenomenon in the immediate vicinity. Bearing in mind that this seemingly real, but impossible, phenomenon could only be due to a fortuitous concatenation of actual occurrences, Nora was not disturbed in her mind. Leaving her cart some little distance up the road, in order that she might not be seen in the undignified position of pushing it, she walked into Klingenspiel's front yard, bearing her gift.

The two-story white house of Wilhelm Klingenspiel seemed to be deserted. Despite the genial season, every door was shut, and so was every window, so far as Nora could see, for if any windows were open down stairs, at least the blinds were shut. There were no blinds in the second story. Looking around in no little disappointment, she was astonished to see a row of sheds and fences in rear of the house had been demolished as if struck by a cyclone and that a goodly sized barn had departed from its normal position and with frame intact was lying on its side like a toy barn tipped over by a child. As she was gazing upon this ruinage and striving to conjecture what had caused it, she heard a voice, muffled and strange, yet distinctly audible, saying:

"Ribot is running amuck, Ribot is running amuck," and looking up she beheld, darkly visible against the panes of an upper story window, a human form. As she looked, the form disappeared and presently a person rushed from the front door, hauled her into the house and upstairs, where she found herself still holding her cabbage and observing a short man of a full habit, with a round moon face, illuminated by a large pair of spectacles that sustained themselves with difficulty upon a very snub nose. He was nearly bald, yet nevertheless of a kindly, studious, and astute appearance. One did not need to look twice to see that Wilhelm Klingenspiel was a scholar.

"What—what—what is the matter?" exclaimed Nora.

"Ribot is running amuck."

"Who is Ribot?"

Klingenspiel was about to answer, when the whole air was filled with what one would have called a squeal if it had been one fiftieth part so loud, and over a row of willow bushes across the road leapt an astounding great creature, twice as large as the largest elephant, and Nora began to realize that her scientific deductions regarding the phenomenon in the swamp had been utterly erroneous. The creature was of an oblong build, rounded in contour, and its hide was marked by large blotches of black and rufous yellow upon a ground of white. With extreme swiftness the creature scurried down the road, its legs being so short in proportion to its body and moving with such twinkling rapidity that it seemed to be propelled upon wheels. The appearance of this strange monster and the appalling character of its squealing, caused Nora to tremble like a leaf, but the animal having departed, a laudable curiosity made her forget her fears, and she asked:

"What is it?"

"That was Ribot."

"Who and what is Ribot?"

"Ribot was a celebrated French scientist, an authority on the subject of heredity. You doubtless know something of the subject, how certain traits appear in families generation after generation. Accidental traits, if repeated for two or three generations, often become inherent traits. To show you to what a strange extent this is true, I will call your attention to the case of the ducal house of Bethune in France, where three successive generations having had the left hand cut off at the wrist in battle, the next three generations were born without a left hand."

The erudite dissertation of Wilhelm Klingenspiel was here interrupted by the reappearance of the mottled monster, who, with a scream that filled the blue vault of heaven, rushed into the yard and paused before a mighty oak, whose sturdy trunk had stood rooted in that soil before the city of Chicago existed, before the United States was born, when Cahokia was the capital of Illinois and the flag of France waved over the great West. The flash of terrible white teeth showed in the moonlight as the monster gnawed at the base of the tree a few times and with a crash its leafy length lay upon the ground. Contemplating for a brief space the ruin it had wrought, the monster emitted another of its appalling screams and was off once more on its erratic, aimless course.

"What in the world is this awful creature?" cried Nora.

"The subject of heredity," resumed Klingenspiel, "is one of vast importance, and although its principles are well understood, man has hitherto not touched the possibilities that can be accomplished. The span of a man's life is so short that in selecting and breeding choice strains of animals, an individual can see only a comparatively small number of generations succeed each other. Suppose some one family had for two hundred years carried on continuous experiments in breeding any race of animals. What remarkable results would have been attained! Behold what remarkable results are attained in raising varieties of plants, where the swiftness of succeeding generations enables man to accomplish what he seeks in a very short time. Observing the difficulties that confront the animal breeder and wishing to see in my own lifetime certain results that might ordinarily be expected only in a duration of several lifetimes, I sought an animal which came to maturity rapidly, whose generations succeeded each rapidly. At the same time, I wanted an animal comparatively highly organized, a mammal, not a reptile."

At this point, his instructive discourse was interrupted by the reappearance of the monster, which charged into the yard with its nose to the ground, following some scent, sniffing so loudly that the sound was plainly audible despite the closed window. After having hastened about the yard for a few moments it was off up the road to the eastward, still with nose to the ground, until coming to the push cart left at the roadside by Nora, it examined it carefully and then with a sudden access of unaccountable rage, fell upon it and demolished it, beating and chewing it into bits.

Whatever celerity this terrible beast had exhibited before, was now completely eclipsed, as with nose to the ground, it rushed back to the yard, straight to the house, and rearing on its hinder quarters, placed its forelegs on the porch roof, which gave way beneath the ponderous weight. Not disconcerted by the removal of this support, the monster continued to maintain its sitting posture, looking in the window at the terrified persons beyond, snapping and gnashing its huge jaws in a manner terrible to hear and still more terrible to contemplate. Nora was partially reassured by observing that the animal's head was too wide to go through the window, but the hopes thus raised were dashed by Klingenspiel moaning:

"He'll gnaw right through the house, he'll chew right through the roof. He'll get in. He has smelled that big cabbage and he'll get in."

"In that case," remarked Nora, with decision, "I'll not wait for him to come in to get the cabbage, but throw it out to him," and raising the window, thrust out the cabbage, which having caught with a deftness unexpected in a creature of its bulk, the beast retired a short space and proceeded to eat with every appearance of enjoyment.

"In Paris, a few years ago," resumed Klingenspiel, "one of the learned faculty that lend a well deserved renown to the medical department of that ancient institution, the University of Paris, discovered an elixir which used during the period of human growth—and even after—causes the stature to increase. By depositing an increased supply of the matter necessary to the formation of bones, the frame increases and the fleshy covering grows with it. You have doubtless read of this in the papers, as I have seen it mentioned there recently myself———"

"I beg your pardon," interrupted Nora, "but I must know what that monster is. Please do not keep me in suspense any longer."

"Allow me to develop my discourse in its natural sequence," said Klingenspiel. "I learned of this elixir at the time its originator first formulated it and as we were friends, I secured from him the formula——"

"What is that animal?" cried Nora, seizing Klingenspiel's ear with a dexterity born of long experience in educational work, and lifting him slowly toward a position upon the points of his toes.

"A guinea pig, a guinea pig, a guinea pig," howled the student of heredity.

"You guinea, you," exclaimed Nora in incredulous amazement, and yet as she looked at the monster, which having finished the cabbage was crouching contentedly between two huge elms, she was struck by the familiarity of the markings and contour of the tremendous brute. Turning in such wise that of the appendices of his countenance it should be his short and elusive nose instead of his ears presented toward the grasp of the expert in the science of pedagogy, Klingenspiel continued.

"Generations of guinea pigs succeed each other in less than three months. In less than ten months, a pair of guinea pigs become great-grandfather and great-grandmother. In a few years, heredity could here do what a century of breeding horses could not. I treated a pair of young guinea pigs with the elixir. Their growth was wonderful. Their children inherited the size of their parents and to this the elixir added, and so on, cumulatively, for successive generations. I kept only a single pair out of each brood and disposed of that pair as soon as the next generation became grown. I did this partly because I could thus conduct my experiment with greater secrecy. Besides, after the guinea pigs were large enough, I found considerable profit in selling their hides for leather. Unfortunately, the animal is unfit for food. My labors, therefore, were bent upon creating a breed of draught animals, creatures greater than elephants and with the agility of guinea pigs. A team of these guinea pigs would outstrip the fastest horse, though hauling a load of tons. The hide, too, would be extremely valuable. I had at last reached a size beyond which I did not care to go. Ribot and his mate were twice the bulk of elephants. I was now ready to establish a herd. But alas! Two days ago, the mate died. All my labors were for nothing. I had only the one enormous male left. All the connecting links between him and the first small ancestors are gone. But worse. As is often the case with male elephants when the mate dies, Ribot went mad, ran amuck. Hitherto docile and kind, as is the nature of the Cavia cobaya, vulgarly called guinea pig, this evening Ribot became as you have seen him. I have lost my labors. Momentarily I expect to lose my life."

"What's the matter with it now? Look at it, look at it," exclaimed Nora.

Ribot had rolled on his back and after giving a few feeble twitches of his great legs, remained without life, his legs pointing stiffly into the air.

"He is dead," said Klingenspiel, and Nora was unable to tell whether relief and joy or regret and despair predominated in this utterance. "Ribot is dead. Our lives are saved, my experiment is ruined."

Turning toward Nora and scrutinizing her attentively for the first time, he remarked, "How white your face is. The strain has been a dreadful one. It has driven all the color away from you." And then letting his eyes wander over her person until they paused upon her hands resting in the moonlight upon the top of the sash, "and how green your hands are. What can it be? Paris green," he said after a close examination. "It was that which killed Ribot."

"I remember now. Father was sprinkling something on them. It is cabbage worm time."

"I hope you will allow me to call," said Klingenspiel, and Nora graciously assenting, he continued: "I admire your beauty, I admire your many admirable qualities of head and heart, but above all, your decision, your great decision."

"Oh, I don't think I showed much decision just because I threw the cabbage out."

"I referred to your taking my ear and learning, out of its due order in the thesis I was expounding, what manner of beast Ribot was. Ribot killed two of my best African geese. They are, however, still fit for food. I am going to beg your acceptance of one."

"We will have it for dinner to-morrow," said Nora, "and you must come over."

"I shall be pleased to do so," said Klingenspiel, and that was the beginning of a series of visits to the home of Timothy Sullivan that resulted in the marriage of Miss Nora and Wilhelm Klingenspiel. The latter still raises African geese there in the vicinity of Stony Island, but he has made no more experiments with guinea pigs, for his wife will not hear to it.

WHAT BEFELL MR. MIDDLETON BECAUSE OF THE FOURTH GIFT OF THE EMIR.

"What an unpleasant surprise it must have been to Klingenspiel," remarked the emir, when he had completed his narration, "to find all his fine experimenting in the science of heredity merely resulting in nearly accomplishing his own death."

"His experience is not unique," said Mr. Middleton. "There is many an economic, social, political, or industrial change which is inaugurated with the highest hopes only to slay its author in the end."

"We should indeed be careful what waves we set in motion, what forces we liberate," said the emir thoughtfully. "And I have been, too. I have in my possession a constant reminder to be cautious in all my enterprises and undertakings—a monitor forever bidding me think of the consequences of an action, weigh its possible results. It has been in my family for generations. I believe that our house has learned the lesson. I would be glad to give it to some one who, perchance, has not. If it so happens that you are in no need of such a warning, you can perhaps present it to some one else who is." And having said a few words to Mesrour in the language of Arabia, the blackamore brought to him a small case and, from the midst of wrappings of dark green silk, he produced a flask of burnished copper that shone with the utmost brilliance. Handing this to Mr. Middleton and that gentleman viewing it in silence for some time and exhibiting no other emotion than a mild curiosity, largely due to its great weight, a ponderosity altogether out of proportion to its size, the emir exclaimed in a loud voice:

"Do you know what you are holding?" and without waiting for an answer from his startled guest, continued: "Observe the inscription upon the side and the stamp of a signet set upon the seal that closes the mouth."

"I perceive a number of Arabic characters," said Mr. Middleton.

"Arabic!" said the emir. "Hebrew. You are looking upon the seal of the great Solomon himself and that is the prison house of one of the two evil genii whom the great king confined in bottles and cast into the sea. In that collection of chronicles which the Feringhis style the Arabian Nights, you have read of the fisherman who found a bottle in his net and opened it to see a quantity of dark vapor issue forth, which, assuming great proportions, presently took form, coalesced into the gigantic figure of a terrible genii, who announced to his terrified liberator that during his captivity, he had sworn to kill whomsoever let him out of the bottle. This well-known occurrence and stock example of the necessity of being careful of the possible results of one's acts, is so familiar to you as to make its further relation an impertinence on my part. Suffice it to say, in cause you have forgotten a minor detail, there was another genii and another bottle in the sea beside the one found by the fisherman.

"The second bottle in some unknown way came into the possession of Prince Houssein, brother of my great-grandfather's great-grandfather, Nourreddin. This latter prince having need of a certain amount of coin—which was very scarce in Arabia at that time and of great purchasing power, trade being carried on by barter—sent to his brother a request for a loan. The country was in a very disturbed state at that time and Houssein dispatched two messengers at an interval of a day apart. The first of these was robbed and killed. He bore a letter, concealed in his saddle, and the money. The second messenger came in entire safety with that bottle, for no one could be desirous of trifling with anything so fraught with danger as that prison house of the terrible genii. What was the purport of this strange gift has never been guessed. The letter borne by the murdered man doubtless explained. Houssein himself perished of plague before Nourreddin could learn from him."

Mr. Middleton sat holding the enchanted bottle very gingerly. If he had not feared to give offence to the emir, he would have declined the gift, for while not for one moment did he dream that a demoniac presence fretted inside that shining copper, he did believe that it contained some explosive, or what would be more probable, some mephitic substance that gave off a deadly vapor. So, fully resolved to throw the bottle into the river and being very heedful of Achmed's injunction not to let the leaden plug bearing Solomon's seal be removed from the mouth, he placed the gift in his pocket and having thanked the emir for his entertainment and instruction and the gift, he departed.

When Mr. Middleton had stepped into the street, he altered his resolution to immediately dispose of the bottle. He was tired and did not care to walk to the river. Nor did he wish to ride there and alight, spending two car fares to get home. So postponing until the morrow the casting into the Chicago River of the unhappy genii who had once reposed on the bottom of the Persian Gulf, he boarded a car for home.

The bulk and weight of the bottle sagging down his pocket and threatening to injure the set of his coat, Mr. Middleton held his acquisition on his knee. A tall, serious-looking individual was his seat mate, who after regarding the bottle intently for some time, addressed him in a low, but earnest voice.

"Pray pardon my curiosity, but I am going to ask you what that queer receptacle is."

"It is the prison-house of a wicked genii, who was shut therein by King Solomon, the magic influence of whose seal on the plug in the mouth retains him within, for what resistance could the physical force of those copper walls oppose to the strength of that mighty demon?"

Of these words did Mr. Middleton deliver himself, though he knew they must sound passing strange, but on the spur of the moment he could not think what else to say and he hoped that the belief he would create that his mind was affected would relieve him of further questioning, for if put to it and pinned down, what could he say, what plausible account could he give of the bottle? To his surprise, the stranger gave no evidence of other than a complete acceptance of his statement and continuing to make inquiries in a most respectful and courteous way, Mr. Middleton felt he could not be less mannerly himself, and so he related all he knew of the bottle, avowing his belief that it contained some dangerous chemical, such as that devilish corroding stuff known as Greek fire, or some deadly gas.

"Your theory sounds reasonable," said the stranger; "and yet who knows? That inscription certainly is Hebrew. At least, it is neither English nor German. When one has studied psychic phenomena as long as I have, he comes to a point where he is very chary of saying what is not credible. Do I not, time and again, materialize the dead, calling from the winds, the waters, and the earth the dispersed particles of the corporeal frame to reclothe for a little time the spiritual essence? Could not the great Solomon do as much? Is it not possible that that great moral ensamplar, guide, saint, and prophet has imprisoned in that bottle some one of the Pre-Adamite demons? I am not afraid to open the bottle, on the contrary, would be glad to do so. I am a clairvoyant and trance-medium, with materialization as a specialty. My name is Jefferson P. Smitz. Here is my card. I have a seance to-morrow night. Bring your bottle then, and I will open it. The price of admission is," he said, with a glance of tentative scrutiny, "one dollar," at which information Mr. Middleton, looking unresponsive, uninterested, not to say sulky, he continued: "but as you will bring such an important and interesting contribution to the subject of inquiry for the evening, we will make the admission for you only fifty cents, fifty cents."

On the following evening, Mr. Middleton and his bottle sat among a circle of some thirty persons who were gathered in the gloomy, lofty-ceiled parlor of Mr. Smitz. Before forming the circle, Mr. Smitz had addressed the company in a few well-chosen words, saying that a like purpose had brought all there that night, that as votaries of science and devotees of truth and persons of culture and refinement, mutual acquaintance could not but be pleasant as well as helpful, enabling those who sat together while witnessing the astounding and edifying phenomena they were soon to behold, to discuss these phenomena with reciprocal benefit—in view of all this, he hoped everybody would consider themselves introduced to everybody else.

Mr. Middleton, quickly inspecting the assemblage, whom he doubtless with great injustice denominated a crowd of sober dubs and solemn stiffs, so maneuvered that when all had drawn their chairs into a circle, a man deaf in the right ear sat at his left, while at his right sat a tall young lady, who though slightly pale was of an interesting appearance, notwithstanding. The somewhat tragic cast of her large and classic features was intensified by a pair of great mournful eyes and a wistful mouth, the whole framed in luxuriant masses of black hair, and altogether she was a girl whom one would give a second and third glance anywhere.

It developing in their very first exchange of remarks that she had never been present at a seance and that she could not look forward to what they were about to witness without great trepidation, Mr. Middleton offered to afford her every moral support and such physical protection as one mortal can assure another when facing the unknown powers of another world. At the extinguishment of the gas, he took her left hand, and finding it give a faint tremor, he took the other and was pleased to note that, so far as her hands gave evidence, thereupon her fears were quite allayed.

A breeze, chill and dank as the breath of a tomb, blew upon the company, and from the deep darkness into which they all stared with straining, unseeing eyes, came the solemn sound of Mr. Smitz, speaking hurriedly in somber tones in some sonorous unknown tongue, and low rustlings and whirrs and soft footfalls and faint rattlings that grew stronger, louder, each moment, swelling up into the stamp of a mailed heel and the clangor of arms as Mr. Smitz scratched a match and the light of a gas jet glanced upon helmet, corslet, shield, and greaves of a brazen-armored Greek warrior, standing in the middle of the circle, alive, in full corporeal presence!

"Leonidas, hero of Thermopylæ!" shouted Mr. Smitz, and then continued at a conversational pitch, "if any of you wish to speak to him in his own language, you have full permission to do so."

Those present lacking either the desire to accost the dread presence, or a command of the ancient Greek, after a bit Mr. Smitz turned off the gas and the noises that had heralded the visitant's appearance began in reverse order, and at their cease, the gas being turned on again, there was the circle quite bare of any evidence that a Greek warrior in full panoply had but now stood there.

At these prodigies, the young lady trembled, but you could have applied all sorts of surgical devices for measuring nerve reaction to Mr. Middleton from the crown of his head to where his parallel feet held between them the copper bottle, and not have detected a tremor.

Mr. Smitz was reaching up to extinguish the gas once more, when a big, athletic blonde man, whose appearance and garb proclaimed him an Englishman, interrupted him.

"I am going to request you to materialize the spirit with whom I wish to converse, the next time. I have to catch a train at eleven and there are a number of things I would like to do before that. Yesterday, you promised me that you would materialize him first thing."

"Yesterday," said Mr. Smitz with a slight hauteur, "I could not look forward and see that I was to have such a large and cultivated gathering. You cannot, sir, ask to have your own mere personal business, for business it is with you, take precedence of the scientific quests of all these other ladies and gentlemen. I have planned to materialize men of many nations, with whom all may converse if they please; Confucius, the great Chinese; Cæsar, the great Roman; Mohammed, the great Turk; Powhattan, the great Indian, and others. Your business must wait."

"My friends," said the Englishman, appealing to the assemblage, "I throw myself upon your good nature. My grandfather was the owner of a small estate in Ireland. In a rebellion, the Irish burned every building on the place and it has since been deserted. He had buried a sum of money before he fled during the rebellion and we have a chart telling where it was buried. But the chart referred to buildings and trees that were subsequently utterly destroyed. We have no marks to guide us. I am sadly in need of money. My grandfather's ghost could tell me where the treasure is. I shall suffer financial detriment if I do not catch the train at eleven and must attend to several matters before that. You have heard my case. May I not ask you all to grant me the indulgence of having my affair disposed of now?"

Mr. Middleton and several others were about to endorse the justice of the Englishman's request, when Mr. Smitz hastily forestalled them by saying that all should be heard from and turning to four personages who sat together at a point where the line of chairs of the circle passed before a large and mysterious cabinet set in the corner of the wall, and asking their opinion, they all four in one voice began to object to any alteration of the program of the evening, adverting somewhat to the Boer War, the oppressions in Ireland, and to the Revolution and the War of 1812. When they had done, there was no one who cared to say a word for the Englishman or an Englishman, and Mr. Smitz announced that Confucius would be the next materialization and that all might address him in his native tongue. Of this permission, a small red-head gentleman, whose demeanor advertised him to be in a somewhat advanced state of intoxication, availed himself and remarked slowly:

"Hello, John. Washee, washee? Sabe how washee? Wlanter be Melican man?"

To this the great sage vouchsafed no reply save a contemptuous stare, and the red-headed gentleman observed that doubtless the Chinese language had changed a good deal in two thousand years. All languages did.

From out the darkness under whose cover the Chinaman was modestly divesting himself of his body, came the voice of Mr. Smitz, rich, unctuous, saying:

"The next visitant will be from that great race we all admire so much, the noble race which has done so much to build up this country, which in every field of American endeavor has been a guiding star to us all. It gives me great pleasure to tell you that our next visitant from the world beyond is that great soldier, statesman, and patriot, King Brian Boru."

"Who the devil wants to see that or any other paddy?" exclaimed the voice of the Englishman, choleric, savage. "Let me out of this blarsted, cheating hole. Who wants to see one of that race of quarrelsome, thieving, wretched rapscallions?"

Whack! Smash! Bang! Crash! The assemblage was thrown into a pitiable state of terror by a most extraordinary combat and tumult taking place somewhere in the circle. The remonstrances of Mr. Smitz and the oaths of the Englishman rose against the general din of the expostulations of the men and cries of the women. Match after match was struck by the men, only to be blown out by some mysterious agency, after giving momentary glimpses of the Englishman astride of a man on the floor, pummelling him lustily, while Mr. Smitz pulled at the Englishman's shoulders. At length the noise died away, the sound of some one remonstrating, "let me at him oncet, let me at the spalpeen, he got me foul," coming back from some remote region of the atmosphere, as under the compelling force of the will of the great Smitz, the bodily envelope of the Irish hero was dissipated and his soul went back to the beyond.

Then did a match reach the gas without being blown out. Beneath the chandelier stood Mr. Smitz and the four personages who had sat before the cabinet and had views on the Boer War.

"What an awful, sacrilegious thing you have done," exclaimed Mr. Smitz. "You have struck the dead."

"He hit me first."

"Your remarks about the Irish angered him. He could not restrain himself."

"Well, he couldn't whip me. Next time you materialize him, he'll show a black eye. Let me out of here, you cheat, you imposter, you and your pals, or I'll fix you as I did Brian Boru."

Though the company did not take the Englishman's view, they were all anxious to go. They were quite unstrung by what had occurred, this combat between the living and the dead. They looked with horrified awe at the spot where it had taken place. There stood the living combatant, still full of the fire of battle. Him whom he had fought was gone on the winds to the voiceless abodes of the departed, a breath, a shadow, a sudden chill on the cheek and nothing more. For a brief space resuming his old fleshly habitue, with it had come the cholers and hatreds of the flesh and once more he avenged his country's wrongs.

"Say," said the Englishman, with a malign look on his face, as he paused in the door, "if you've got that mick patched up any down in the kitchen, I'll give him another chance, if he wishes. Tell him to pick a smaller man next time."

To this, Mr. Smitz made no reply, but flashed a look that would have frozen any one less insolent and truculent than the Englishman.

All this time Mr. Middleton had been very agreeably employed in a corner of the room, for the young lady in an access of terror had thrown herself into his arms and there she had remained during the whole affrighting performance. To forerun any possible apprehension that he was going to extricate himself and leave her, he held her with considerable firmness, whispering encouragement into her ear the while. Preparing to accompany her home, he had almost left the room before he bethought him of the copper bottle, which he had abandoned when springing up to get the young lady out of the circle and away from danger. He soon found it lying against the wall, whither it had rolled or been kicked during the melee.

The young lady continuing to be in a somewhat prostrated state after her late experience, on the way home Mr. Middleton supported her by his right arm about her waist, while she found further stay by resting her left arm across his shoulders, she being a tall young lady. Their remaining hands met in a clasp of cheer and encouragement on his part, of trusting dependence on hers. Arriving at her door in this fashion, it was but natural for Mr. Middleton—who was a very natural young man—to clasp her in a good-night embrace, but upon essaying to put the touch of completion to these joys which a kiss would give, she drew away her head, saying:

"Why, how dare you, sir! I never met you before. Why, I haven't even been formally introduced to you."

Mr. Middleton humbly pleading for the salute, she continued to express her surprise that he should prefer such a request upon no acquaintance at all, that he should even faintly expect her to grant it, and so on, all the while leaning languishing upon his breast with all her weight. Whereupon Mr. Middleton lost patience and with incisive sarcasm he began:

"One would think that you who refuse this kiss were not the girl who stands here within my arms, my lips saying this into her ears, her cheek almost touching mine. Doubtless it is some one else. Pray tell me, what great difference is there between kissing a stranger and hugging him."

At these brutal, downright words, leaving the poor young thing nothing to say, no little pretence even to herself that she had guarded the proprieties, had comported herself circumspectly, leaving her with not even a little rag of a claim that she had conducted herself with seemly decorum, she sprang from him and began to cry. Whatever the cause, Mr. Middleton could not look upon feminine unhappiness with composure and here where he was himself responsible, he was indeed smitten with keen remorse and hastening to comfort her, gathered her into his arms and there he was abasing and condemning himself and telling her what a dear, nice girl she was—and kissing away her tears.

"Let me give you a piece of advice," he said, fifteen minutes later, as he was about to release her and depart. "It is not best ever to let a man hug you. Never," he said, pausing to imprint a lingering kiss upon the girl's yielding lips, "never let a man kiss you again until that moment when you shall become his affianced wife."

Mr. Middleton departed in that serene state of mind which the consciousness of virtue bestows, for he had given the young woman valuable advice that would doubtless be of advantage to her in the future and he reflected upon this in much satisfaction as he fared away with the eyes of the young woman watching him from where she looked out of the parlor window.

Reaching into his right coat pocket to transfer the copper bottle to the opposite pocket, in order that his coat might not be pulled out of shape, as he grasped the neck, one of his fingers went right into the mouth! The seal of Solomon was gone! A less resolute and quick-witted person might have been alarmed, but reasoning that the seal must have been knocked off during the fight at Mr. Smitz's and nothing had happened since, he boldly examined the bottle. He could see a white substance as he looked into it, and by the aid of a stick he fished out a wad of wool tightly stuffed in the neck. A metallic chinking followed the removal of the wadding and set his heart thumping rapidly. He looked up and down the street. No one in sight. He tilted the bottle up to the light of a street lamp and saw a yellow gleam. He shook it and into his hands flowed a stream of gold sequins! He could not sufficiently admire the ruse of Prince Houssein. Money on the first messenger there had been none.

In a center more given to numismatics, or had he been willing to wait and sell the coins gradually, Mr. Middleton might have secured more than he did for the gold pieces, all coined at Bagdad in the early caliphates and very valuable. But he disposed of them in a lump to a French gentleman on La Salle Street for fourteen hundred and twenty-five dollars.

Calling on the young lady of Englewood within the next few days, he made no reference to these events, though she asked him several times during the evening what he had been doing lately. He did, however, hint at having profited by a certain fortunate "deal," as he called it, but not a word did he say concerning the mournful girl or anything remotely connected with her.

Hesitating to hurt the emir's feelings by exposing the obtuseness of his ancestor Noureddin and the foolish superstition of his descendants ever since, Mr. Middleton said nothing of these transactions when once more he sat in the presence of the urbane and accomplished prince of the tribe of Al-Yam. Having handed him a bowl of delicately flavored sherbet, the emir began the narration of The Pleasant Adventures of Dr. McDill.

THE PLEASANT ADVENTURES OF DR. MCDILL.

IT WAS twelve o'clock on a blustery winter night and Dr. James McDill was where a married man of forty ought to be at such an hour in that season, sleeping soundly by the side of his beloved wife. But his wife was not sleeping. At the stroke of the hour, she had suddenly awoke from refreshing slumber and become aware of sounds as of persons moving softly about the room, and after a little, seeing against the windows faintly illuminated by a distant street light, two dark figures, she perceived her ears had not deceived her. Shaking her husband unavailingly for a considerable time, in her terror she finally cast discretion to the winds and shouted:

"Burglars, Jim, burglars!"

Hardly had these words ceased, when the electric lights were turned on and Dr. McDill sat up in bed to find himself staring into the muzzles of three revolvers, held by two masked men, who stood looking over the footboard. Bidding them move at their peril, the man with two revolvers remained to guard the doctor and his wife, while the other began to ransack the room. As he did so, he carried on an easy, if not eloquent, dissertation upon the rights of man and the iniquitous conditions which made it necessary for the poor and oppressed to obtain by force, if they obtained at all, any share in the privileges and riches of the wealthy. As he discoursed, at times carried away by his theme, he gave over his search and paused to enforce his points with earnest gestures. This caused the other robber some disquietude and he cursed his compatriot and the doctor and his wife with a use of epithets that will not bear repeating and which showed him to be none other than a low ruffian. At last all the treasure in the room being taken and the doctor being forced to accompany them and disclose the repository of other valuables, the robbers took their departure.

Some weeks after this, two persons suspected of being responsible for certain robberies were taken into custody and the doctor called into court to identify them if possible.

"I noticed," said he, "that the shorter of the two masked men was prone to gesticulation and that he had a fashion of holding his arms close to his body, as if tied at the elbows, and with hands fully open, fingers apart, thumbs extended, and palms upward, waving his forearms——"

At this juncture, the smile on the face of the defendant's counsel, occasioned by thus putting his client upon his guard, was dispelled by an angry exclamation from the person in question, and denying with some loquacity and even more vociferation that he ever made such a gesture, at the close of his statement, behold, he made the gesture!

By the doctor's testimony was a chain of incriminating evidence established that led to a sentence of ten years' imprisonment being imposed upon the robbers. When he had heard the sentence, he of the gestures turned fiercely toward the doctor and cried:

"You'll be killed for this, like other dogs before you for the same cause. If you're not killed before I am discharged or escape, I'll kill you. But I am only one of many, a tried band who avenge;" and hereupon he smote the rail in front of him, "Knock, knock—knock; knock, knock—knock." And from several parts of the silent room came answers, faint, but distinct, two quick taps, a pause, and a third, then all repeated. "Tap, tap—tap; tap, tap—tap."

The evidence of confederates, the quick response to the appeal of their comrade, the taps that came from everywhere and nowhere, manifestation of the desperate men surrounding him, might well have daunted the soul of any man. Three sentences had been pronounced that day, a term of years upon Jerry McGuire and Barry O'Toole, but death upon James McDill. You may depend upon it that the doctor was none the more reassured when on the morrow he learned that McGuire and O'Toole had escaped. With their anger and resentment yet hot within them, these men would doubtless at once set about to encompass his destruction, and he knew that when once one of these societies had decreed the death of a person who balked or incensed them, every endeavor was used to put the decree into effect. But, after a little, he took courage from the very fact that was most threatening. If these men, these desperate and despicable scoundrels, could escape from the barriers of stone and steel and the guardians that surrounded them, why might not he fight for his life and win in the struggle which both reason and instinct told him was inevitable?

That those he loved most might not be involved in the perils he felt certain he was about to encounter and that his resolution and his movements might not be hampered by their presence and their fears, he found means to persuade his wife to take the children for a visit to their grandfather, and setting his affairs in order and providing himself with two revolvers, a bowie knife, and an Italian stiletto, he even began to look forward to the approaching struggle with something of that pleasure which man experiences in the anticipation of any contest; and there is indeed a certain keen zest in playing the game where one's stake is one's life.

On the evening of the day of his wife's departure, he was called to assist in an operation at a hospital with which he had once been connected, and unexpected complications arising, it was not until two in the morning that he started away. His man and carriage, that he had ordered to await him, had gone. The night was mild and it must have been weariness or restiveness, that had caused the departure. Although some distance lay between the hospital and his home, he started afoot. Not a soul was to been seen in the street, which, thanks to the light of the moon late rising in its last quarter, lay visible to his sight. As he passed an alleyway, shortly after leaving the hospital, his attention was attracted by the sound of snores, and he discovered a man whose features were well shrouded in the upturned collar of an ulster, seated with his back against a house wall, asleep. The man stirred uneasily as he bent over him, but thinking it best not to disturb him, the doctor passed on. As he did so, he became conscious that the snores had ceased, and looking back, he beheld the man walk drowsily across the sidewalk and finally stand gazing in the direction of the hospital. The doctor began to hasten his steps, but ever and anon glancing back, and presently he saw the man was now looking after him, that he leaned to the right and leaned to the left, and stooped down in his scrutinizing. Suddenly the man reached forward with a cane, smote the sidewalk, "rap, rap—rap; rap, rap—rap," and taken up on either side of the way, louder and louder as it came up the street toward the now fleeing doctor, from sequestered nooks between buildings, ran the fateful, hurrying volley of "rap, rap—rap; rap, rap—rap." The last raps came right behind the doctor's heels at the mouth of an alley he was clearing at a bound, and glancing back, he saw a succession of men hurrying silently after him at all speed. He was encumbered with a long ulster, while his pursuers, if they had worn overcoats, had now cast them aside. The man just behind, apparently did not wish to close in alone, preferring to allow others to catch up and assist him, and at the second block the doctor could hear two pairs of heels behind him and a third pair just beyond. The pursuers were gaining. Though he would have to pause to do it, he must throw off his overcoat. At the third corner, he tore at the long garment, it swung under his feet, and he pitched headlong——. He heard a cry of savage joy and a rush of feet, a sudden great soft whirr, and he arose to see an automobile halted between him and his pursuers. A gentleman of a rotund person, clothed in correct evening dress and whose speech was of a thickness to indicate recent indulgence in intoxicating liquors, alighted from the carriage.

"I do not believe thish ish the place. No, thish ish not the place I told you to come to, driver. I'm glad it isn't anyway, as I'm afraid we're too drunk to sing a serenade. Here's another man as's drunk, too. So drunk he fell down on hisself. Couldn't leave him here. Never go back on a man as is drunk. Get in brother. Take you home with us. Get in."

It is needless to say that Dr. McDill responded to his invitation with the greatest alacrity and gratitude. For the first time did the rotund gentleman become aware that there were other persons present. Some four of the doctor's pursuers had now gathered at the curb of the crossing and the rest were coming thither, though with no great haste, for they were gentry to whom caution was second nature and it was by no means certain what the arrival of the automobile might portend. The four at the curb, deterred from retreat by that sense of shame which is not entirely absent even in the lowest and most depraved, were now insistently giving their rap to incite their comrades to hasten. The rotund gentleman walked around to that side of the carriage and gazed at them with some degree of interest and curiosity. "Rap, rap—rap; rap, rap—rap," went the sticks of the four and down the street came answering raps and soon the four were joined by two more.

"Don't let him go now, we've almost got him. We'd had him, if Red hadn't gone to sleep and let him get by. Come on, come on."

The six rushed at the carriage, whereat the rotund gentleman, with an agility not to be looked for in one of his contour and condition, received the foremost with smash, smash—smash, in each eye and on the nose, and the second likewise, when bidding the driver be off, he leaped into the carriage with his comrades. A single bullet whistled after them as they whirled away.

"Rap, rap—rap. I rapped 'em," said the rotund gentleman. "I always did hate a knocker."

With your permission I will here interpolate the remark that the further adventures of the eminent surgeon with the mysterious confederacy that sought his life, bore evidence that these depraved and ruffianly men were not without a certain rude artistic temperament as well as a tinge of romance, and a dramatic sense that many who write for the stage might well envy them.

The elation of the doctor over his escape from the toils of the thieves was not of long duration. His breakfast was interrupted by a call to the telephone and over the wires came to his startled ears a hollow "knock, knock—knock; knock, knock—knock." At his office door down town softly came "tap, tap—tap; tap, tap—tap," and snatch the door open as hastily as he might, he saw nothing, heard nothing, heard nothing but the electric bells on the floors above and floors below calling for the elevator: "buzz, buzz—buzz; buzz, buzz—buzz." He walked along State Street at the busy hour of noon and all about him in the throngs was the dull impact of canes upon the pavement, "thud, thud—thud; thud, thud—thud." As he rode home in the street car at nightfall, back of him in the train at street corner after corner he heard passengers jingle the bell for stopping, "ding, ding—ding; ding, ding—ding."

Although Dr. McDill was a man of great native resolution and intrepid in the face of known and seen dangers, the horrors of the invisible forces of death everywhere surrounding him so wore at his soul that he returned down town and spent the night at a hotel. On the morrow, he severely condemned himself for this yielding to fear, for on the front steps of his house lay the dead form of his great watch dog, Jacques. There were evidences of a struggle in which the assailants had not been unscathed. Bits of cloth lay about and examining the stains of blood that plentifully blotched the walk, he discovered that some of it was human blood.

"Ah," he said, in deep self-reproach, "if I had stayed here as I should, I would have been able to fight with poor Jacques and brought low some of my enemies. How easily I could have fired from the upper windows as Jacques made their presence known. It is evident that the noise of the struggle was so great that the fiends were afraid to continue the attack and ran away."

Philosophers and poets have found a theme for dissertation in the fact that the dog leaves his own kindred to dwell with man and fights them in behalf of his master. It has ever seemed to me that this were but half of the tale, for full many a man loves his dog better than the rest of mankind, and so the devotion of the race of dogs finds return and recompense. Outside his own family, there was no living thing in the city of Chicago which had so dwelt in the affections of Dr. McDill as the dog Jacques. Of the truth of this, he had had but dim realization until now and he was like to burst with sorrow and with hatred of the vile beings who had marked him and his for slaughter. Lifting the stiff form of his humble comrade, for the first time did he observe a poniard thrust in the poor beast's throat. The blade impaled a piece of paper and upon it was written the word "Knock."

"Knock!" cried the doctor: "but henceforth it shall be I that knock. Hasten the time when we may meet, malignant knaves. Never again shall I avoid you. Henceforth, I go about my business as before, for it is thus that I may expect the sooner to encounter you."

An urgent matter would require the doctor's presence in the municipality of Evanston that night. He could not expect to return before twelve o'clock in the morning and of this informing the cook, who in the temporary reduction of the family carried on the household without the aid of a second girl, he departed northward. It was past the hour of one when he let himself in the front door of his residence. A pleasant savor of various viands saluted his nostrils and in the drawing-room he observed that the chairs and tables had all been thrust against the wall as if to clear the floor for dancing. In the dining-room, the evidence of recent festivity was complete, for the table was covered with the remnants of a sumptuous repast. No words were needed to tell him that Olga Blomgren, the cook, had taken advantage of the foreknowledge of his absence to entertain a wide circle of friends; but here indeed was a mystery. Why had she not set everything in order and removed all traces of the entertainment? He moved toward the kitchen in wonder and—his heart stood still. The beams of the lamp held above his head were shot back by the gleam of blue and white satin, his wife's favorite ball dress on the kitchen floor. But it was not his wife's fair hair and snowy shoulders that, rising out of the glistening blue and white, were striped with a glistening red, but the snowy shoulders and fair hair of poor Olga Blomgren. Thus had she paid for her hour of magnificence. Thus had death cut her down because the maid's form was of the same statuesque beauty as her mistress's. Tenderly the doctor stooped to lift up the dead girl, stricken in her mistress's stead. There was a poniard in her throat, and it impaled a piece of paper upon which was written "Knock."

"Knock, knock—" the next knock would be upon his own heart.

Whatever design the doctor had held of not appealing to the police for protection against his invisible foes, his affairs had now reached a point where the intervention of the officers of the law could no longer be avoided. Poor Jacques could be consigned to earth without the intervention of priest or police, but the murder of Olga was a matter for official investigation. With that crafty and subtle way the astute sleuths of the Chicago constabulary have of informing the public through the intermediary of the press of all measures projected against evil-doers, of moves to be made, of arrests to be attempted, all citizens were in possession of the fact that owing to the startling plot just brought to light, all gatherings and coteries of men, especially at late hours, were to be watched, investigated, and made to give accounts of themselves. Dr. McDill fumed at the turn affairs had taken. That the confederacy of thieves would abandon their attempts upon his life, was not to be dreamed of. But they would forego the pleasure of witnessing his death in the presence of all assembled together. They would now delegate the attack to a single individual, and in event of his death, he could hope to carry with him but one of his enemies.

Again was Dr. McDill called to the hospital for a night operation. Leaving his driver without, he cautioned him.

"August, I don't want you to be fooled the way you were before. If any man comes out of the hospital and says I send word for you to drive home without waiting for me, pay no attention to him. Take no orders from anybody but me."

"All right. They can't fool me vonce again already."

But when a cab drove up and let out a tall gentleman in a silk hat, who went into the hospital, and after a little the cab driver, a friendly and talkative person of Irish extraction, offered August a flask full of a beverage also of Irish extraction, August took a drink.

"He told me not to take no orders yet already from nobody but him. But he didn't say nothin' about takin' a drink vonce."

"Take a drink twice, then, Hans," said the person of Irish extraction, "already, yet, and by and by, too."

It was all of four hours later that Dr. McDill stepped out of the hospital door. He paused under the light of the globe over the porch and examining a large bag of water-proof silk, he thrust therein a sponge upon which he poured the contents of a small phial, after which, seeing that a noose of string that closed the mouth of the bag was not entangled, he strode briskly toward his buggy. The side curtains were on and consequently the interior was in a dark shadow. Pausing a moment on the step, as if to arrange his overcoat, he made a quick, dexterous movement toward the person in the carriage and, throwing the bag over his head, pulled the noose. A terrific blow struck the doctor in the breast, but the arm that struck it fell powerless before it could be repeated and the striker lurched forward on the dashboard in the utter limpness of complete insensibility.

"It is not August," said the doctor, straightening up the hooded figure and taking the reins. "How well was my precaution taken! I believe that was the last knock that any member of that band of diabolical assassins will ever strike."

In the private laboratory of his own home, the doctor sat facing his captive, whom, after binding hand and foot, he had restored to his senses. The outlaw was the first to break the silence.

"You've got me and you think you'll do me," said the outlaw, with a succession of oaths and vile epithets it would be needless as well as improper for me to repeat. "But if you harm me, my friends will more than pay you up for it, just as they have everybody that crossed them."

"Your friends are of a mind to kill me, whatever befall. Sparing or killing you, will in nowise affect their purpose. Whatever may come to-morrow, to-night you must obey my commands."

"I won't do a thing you tell me to. I don't have to, see? My friends will look for you just as soon as I don't turn up, and it will go hard with you."

"Just as soon as you do not turn up with the news you have killed me. We'll see whether you will do what I tell you to."

"You dassen't kill me. You're afraid to kill me. My friends would fix you and the law would get you, if they did not."

"Your profession relies upon the forbearance and softheartedness of the public. You know that those you rob hesitate to shoot. No such hesitation hampers you. It is part of your stock in trade to keep the public terrorized. You kill all who disobey your orders, for if people began to resist you successfully you must needs go out of business. Did all put aside their repugnance to shed blood and kill your kind as they would wolves, we would have no more of you."

"You dassen't kill me, you dassen't kill me," cried the robber. It was the snarl of the wild beast, hopelessly held in the toils.

"It is true that I hesitate to kill. I am not proud of this hesitation, for the trend of the best medical and sociological thought is now toward the execution of all degenerates and criminals, that they may not contaminate the race with descendants. However, my office is to save life and I cannot do otherwise. But I am a surgeon, and every day I do things in the effort to save and prolong life that to a layman are repulsive and awful, more revolting to him than the sight of bloodless death itself. From the taking of human life I draw back. But no repugnance, no horror, unsteadies my hand elsewhere. The end of the crimes of your devilish confederacy has come. The law has not restrained you, could not. Your own unparalleled wickedness has delivered you into my hands. Many a man have you brought low, many a family have you desolated. Widows and orphans cry out against you, and not in vain. I shall so knock your gang that never again shall one of you harm even the weakest. You shall all live, but it shall be your prayer, if you black hearts can utter prayer, that you be dead."

The outlaw's tongue moved thickly in a mouth that dried suddenly at these solemn words of the doctor. "You can't do it, you can't do it, you can't do it, you duffer———" and his voice rumbled on in a long string of imprecations.

The doctor seized him and carrying him to the cellar, lay him against the coal bin. Then the captive heard him in a room above engaged upon some sort of carpentry, and whether it was the captive's imagination, or design of the doctor, or whether unconsciously the doctor's mind had become possessed, the sounds of the hammer as it drove nails and struck pieces of wood into place echoed in the cellar; "knock, knock—knock; knock, knock—knock." Soon the stairs groaned under the weight of the doctor carrying some great contrivance, and the outlaw found himself lying stretched out upon some sort of operating chair, his ankles held in a pair of stocks below, his outstretched arms held by the wrists in a pair of stocks above. All was black in the cellar, all but where a single blood red bar of light from the open door of the furnace fell upon the doctor turning at the winch of the bed of torture upon which lay the robber.

Hardly ten turns did he make, for at the first little twinges of pain, premonishing the agonies to come, the caitiff chattered in terror promises to do all the doctor should order, and so was released. Cringing and fawning, the outlaw heard what he was required to do. He was to write a letter. In this, he was to tell of the method of his capture. He was to say he was confined in a second-story room, feet and hands shackled, and that he was also chained to a staple in the floor. (That this all might be true, the doctor took him to a second-story room and so fettered him.) He found himself able to use his hands to write, and, happily, discovered writing material and stamps upon a table. He would write a letter and throw it on the porch below, where perhaps the postman would find it and send it to its destination. He asked help. His friends must come that night. The doctor would be on guard, and who could say he would not call in others? The doors and windows were all well secured, all but a cellar window on the east side. (Of this, the doctor informed him, that he, the doctor, might not be guilty of instigating the writing of anything that was false in any particular.) They must enter by this window. The door leading above stairs from the cellar could be easily forced and the noise thus occasioned could not be heard outside of the house. They must come at two in the morning. Come before another dawn, as the doctor was going to hold him one day before turning him over to the police, hoping the gang would do something to involve themselves in some way they would not if the police were after them with a hue and cry.

The outlaw wrote the letter as ordered, addressed it to Barry O'Toole, and threw it out of the window. It fell beyond the porch, on the ground. But this the doctor remedied by hiring a small boy for ten cents to pick it up and put it in a mail box. After which, the doctor betook himself to the nearest extensive hardware establishment.

At two o'clock the next morning, the beams of a dark lantern shone athwart the darkness of the cellar of Dr. McDill's residence.

"It's all right, boys. I can smell escaping gas, but it's all right. There's nobody in there. Now for the doctor. We'll kill him and all who are in there with him, and burn the house," said a voice behind the lantern, and one after another, eleven burly men dropped into the cellar through the narrow east window high in the wall. As the feet of the last man struck the ground, there was a sound as of a rope jerked by some one in the orifice by which they had just entered, and they heard two succeeding crashes within the cellar, followed by the slam of an iron shutter over the window. There was a sound of a spasmodic rush upon the cellar stairs and a beating upon the door, and then a succession of softer sounds, as of men rolling down stairs, and then silence.

A match was struck upon the outside of the iron shutter. It revealed the face of Dr. McDill, lighting a cigar.

"The gas alone would have been almost sufficient. But when all those bottles of ether and chloroform broke—— I had better open the window so it will work off and I can get them out. I will write to my wife to stay away two months longer. Olga is dead and Kate is gone. I'll discharge August to-morrow, as he deserves. The field is clear."

One morning, as Hans Olson, cook of the King Olaf Magnus, staunch schooner engaged in the shingle trade between Chicago and the city of Manistee, state of Michigan, on this particular morning lying in the Chicago River—on this morning, as Mr. Olson was pouring overboard some dishwater, preparing the breakfast for the yet sleeping crew, he was horrified to see floating in the current that would eventually carry them past the great city of St. Louis, twelve naked human arms. Despite his horror and alarm at this grewsome array of severed members, he noted that so far as he could observe, they were all left arms, forearms, disjointed at the elbows. Subsequent examination but added to the mystery. It was no trick of medical students intended to set the town agog. They were not dissecting subjects, but limbs lately taken from living bodies, and they were detached with the highest skill known to the art of chirurgery. The town talked and it was a day's wonder, but the solving of the mystery proving impossible, it was passing into tradition when all were horrified anew to hear that Johannes Klubertanz, a member of the great and honest German-American element, while walking through Lincoln Park early one morning, stumbled over some objects which, upon examination, proved to be twelve human forearms, right forearms!

Again were the wisest baffled in even guessing at this riddle, as they were a third time, when one Prosper B. Shaw came with the story that while rowing down in the drainage canal, he had come upon, floating gently along, dissevered at the knee joint, twelve human legs!

The whole community shuddered at the dark secret hidden in their midst, but at last came the answer, yet not the answer. Of all strange crews that mortal sight has gazed upon, that was the strangest, that dozen men who out of nowhere appeared suddenly in the streets one morning, armless all, all with wooden left legs. Their story you would ask in vain, for just the little chord by which the tongue forms intelligible words was gone. Their babblings came just to the border of articulate speech, but not beyond. Torrents of half-formed words they poured forth, but only half-formed, and to their mouthed jabber the crowd listened without understanding. Did you thrust a pencil in their jaws and bid them write their tale? Gone was some little muscle that grips the jaws and the pencils lolled between teeth that could not nip them. And as for their lips, oh, their mouths, their mouths! Such an example of the chirurgery that has to do with the altering of the human face had never before been witnessed, for nature had never made those faces. One such countenance she might have made in cruel sport, but never twelve, and twelve altogether, as like as peas in a pod, twelve human jack o'lanterns, twelve travesties upon humanity's front. Howsoever they might once have looked, not even their own mothers could know them now. Around each eye the same wrinkles led away. On each face was a bulbous nose. But the mouths, oh, the mouths! Each was drawn back over the teeth in a perpetual grin, each was upturned at corners which ended well nigh in the middle of the cheek. Here were the victims of the horrors that had made the city shudder, but dumb and unrecognizable. In all the thousands that looked at them, not one could say he had ever seen them before. In all these thousands, there was not one to whom they could speak. There were their stiff faces, frozen into that terrible perpetual grin, so many idols of wood, save for their eyes, and they were the only things that lived in their dead faces.

Such rudimentary human beings it would be hard to conceive, and so after a while it occurred to some one that the same scientific methods that discover and disclose to us the modes of life, the habits, and even thoughts of primitive and rudimentary man, might be devoted to establishing a means of communication with them and unveil the secret the whole world was eager to know. Accordingly, they were taken to the University of Chicago and turned over to the department of anthropology. The learned expounders of this science were not long in devising a simple means of communication. The twelve unfortunates were seated upon a recitation bench and a doctor of philosophy wrote out an alphabet upon the blackboard.

"One rap of your foot will be A," said the doctor of philosophy. "Two will be B. Two raps, a pause, and one will be C. We will soon learn your story."

At this moment, the reverberations of a prodigious blow upon the door outside echoed through the room, "bang, bang—bang, bang, bang—bang."

Unaccountably startled, as if at the hearing of some portent, the professor stood rooted to the spot for a moment, and then was about to leap to the door, when the simulacrums before him sprang to their feet and with a tremendous stamping, smote their wooden legs upon the floor, "stamp, stamp—stamp, stamp, stamp—stamp."

The professor stared at the twelve mutes. There were their immobile faces, as wooden as their wooden legs, wearing their perpetual grin, but the westering sun shone on their eyes and there he saw an abject, grovelling fear, dreadful to behold, the master passion of twelve souls, slaves to some mysterious will which had just made itself manifest out of the unseen. By what means the will had gained this ascendancy, the terrible disfigurements of their remnants of bodies told only too well, and he who ran could read the utter prostration before the power which in their lives had been the greatest and most terrible in the universe. Again, far off in a distant corridor of the building, slowly rumbled to them: "knock, knock—knock; knock, knock—knock," and the twelve unfortunates, like so many automatons, gave token of their obedience. They had been warned to keep the secret.

And so was foiled the attempts of the learned anthropologists to hold converse with these rudimentary beings. The alphabet of such elaborate devisings went for naught. Never did the twelve persons in the state of primitive culture get further than the letter C: "knock, knock—knock; knock, knock—knock."

WHAT BEFELL MR. MIDDLETON BECAUSE OF THE FIFTH GIFT OF THE EMIR.

"I AM at a loss to understand," said Mr. Middleton, "why you have entitled the narration you have just related, 'The Pleasant Adventures of Dr. McDill.' For to my mind, they seemed anything but pleasant adventures."

"How so?" asked the emir. "Is it not pleasant to thwart the machinations and defeat the evil intentions of the villains such as composed the confederacy that sought the doctor's life? Does there not reside in mankind a sense of justice which rejoices at seeing meted out to wrong-doers the deserts of their crimes?"

To which Mr. Middleton replying with a nod of thoughtful assent, after a proper period of rumination upon the words of the emir, that accomplished ruler continued:

"Despite the boasted protection of the law, how often is a man compelled to rely for his protection upon his own prowess, skill or address. There are many occasions when right under the nose of the police, one saves himself by the resort to physical strength, weapons, or the use of a cajoling tongue. Theoretically, Dr. McDill was amply protected by the mantle of the law. In reality, it was man to man as much as if he had met his foes in the Arabian desert, with none but himself and them and the vultures. Do you go armed?"

"No," replied Mr. Middleton, with a flippant smile; "but I can go pretty fast, and that has heretofore done as well as going armed."

"Young man," said the emir, sternly, "a bullet can outstrip your fleetest footsteps. There may never be but one occasion when you will need a weapon, but on that occasion the possession of the means of protection may spell the difference between life and life."

Hardly had he uttered them, before Mr. Middleton regretted his forward and pert words, for never before had he answered the emir lightly, such was his respect for him as a man of goodly parts and as one set in authority, and such was his gratitude toward him as a benefactor. Stammering forth what was at once an apology and an acknowledgement of the wisdom of what the emir had said, Mr. Middleton began to make preparations to go. But Prince Achmed bade him wait, and saying a few words to Mesrour in the Arabic language, the blackamore brought to him a pair of pistols of a formidable aspect. In sooth, one could hardly tell whether they ought to be called pistols, or culverins. In the shape of the stocks alone could anyone detect that they were pistols. The bore of each was more than an inch in diameter, and the octagonal barrels of thick steel, heavily inlaid with silver, were a foot and a half long. The handles, which were in proportion to the barrels and so long that four hands could grasp them, were so completely covered with an inlay of pearl that no wood was visible. Taking one of them, the emir rammed home a great load of powder, upon which he placed a handful of balls as large as marbles. Having served the second likewise, he handed the pair to Mr. Middleton.

"Take them. Protected by them, you need have little fear. But woe betide the man who stands in front of them, for so wide is the distribution of their charge, that he must be a most indifferent marksman who could not do execution with them."

Thanking the emir for the gift and the entertainment and instruction of his discourse, Mr. Middleton departed. Impressed though he had been by Prince Achmed's counsel and by the lesson to be derived from the recital of the experiences of Dr. McDill, Mr. Middleton did not carry the pistols as he went about his daily vocation. It was impossible to so bestow them about his garments that they did not cause large and unsightly protuberances and to carry them openly was not to be thought of. Their weight, too, was so great that it was burdensome to carry them in any manner. Coming into his room unexpectedly in the middle of the forenoon of the Thursday following the acquisition of the weapons, he surprised Hilda Svenson, maid of all work, in the act of examining one of them, which she had extracted from the place where they lay concealed in the lower bureau drawer beneath a pile of underclothing. With a start of guilty surprise, Hilda let the pistol fall to the floor. Fortunately it did not go off, but nonetheless was he convinced that he ought to dispose of the two weapons, for any day Hilda might shoot herself with one, while on the weekly sheet changing day, Mrs. Leschinger, the landlady, might shoot herself with the other. There was no place in the room where he could conceal them from the painstaking investigations of Hilda and Mrs. Leschinger, and the expedient of extracting the charges not occurring to him, he felt that it was clearly his duty to remove the lives of the two women from jeopardy by disposing of the pistols. He was in truth pained at the necessity of parting with the gifts which the emir had made with such solicitude for his welfare and as some assuagement to this regret he sought to dispose of them as profitably as possible. With this end in view, he made an appointment for a private audience after hours with Mr. Sidney Kuppenheimer, who conducted a large loan bank on Madison Street and was reputed a connoisseur and admirer of all kinds of curios.

On the evening for which he had made the appointment, he set forth, intending to make an early and short call upon his friend Chauncy Stackelberg and wife, before repairing to Mr. Kuppenheimer's place of business. But such was the engaging quality of the conversation of the newly married couple, abounding both in humor and good sense, and so interested was he in hearing of the haps and mishaps of married life, a state he hoped to enter as soon as fortune and the young lady of Englewood should be propitious, that he was unaware of the flight of time until in the midst of a pause in the conversation, he heard the cathedral clock Mrs. Stackelberg's uncle had given her as a wedding present, solemnly tolling the hour of eleven. The hour Mr. Kuppenheimer had named was one hour agone. To have kept the appointment, he should have started two hours before.

Another half hour had flown before Mr. Middleton, having paused to partake of some chow-chow recently made by Mrs. Stackelberg and highly recommended by her liege, finally left the house, carrying a pistol in either hand. The night was somewhat cloudy, but although there was neither moon nor stars, it was much lighter than on some nights when all the minor luminaries are ablaze, or the moon itself is aloft, shining in its first or last quarter, a phenomenon remarked upon by an able Italian scientist in the middle of the last century and by him attributed to some luminous quality that inheres in the clouds themselves. Mr. Middleton was walking along engrossed in thoughts of the scene of domestic bliss he had lately quitted and in dreams of the even more delightful home he hoped to some day enjoy with the young lady of Englewood, when he suddenly became cognizant of four individuals a short distance away, comporting themselves in an unusual and peculiar manner. Cautiously approaching them as quietly as possible, he perceived that it was two robbers despoiling two citizens of their valuables, one pair standing in the middle of the street, one on the sidewalk, the citizens with their hands elevated above their heads in a strained and uncomfortable attitude, while each robber—with back to him—was pointing a revolver with one hand and turning pockets inside out with the other.

With a resolution and celerity that astonished him, as he afterwards dwelt upon it in retrospect, Mr. Middleton rushed silently upon the nearest robber, him in the street, and dealt him a terrible blow upon the head with the barrel of a pistol. Without a sound, the robber sank to the earth, whereupon the citizen, whether he had lost his head through fear, or thought Mr. Middleton a new and more dangerous outlaw, fled away like the wind. Snatching the bag of valuables in the unconscious thief's hands, Mr. Middleton made toward the other robber, who, to his astonishment, hissed without looking around:

"What did you let your man get away for, you fool? Try and make yourself useful somehow. Hold this swag and cover the man, so I can have both hands and get through quick."

Taking the valuables the robber handed him, Mr. Middleton with calmness and deliberation placed them in his pockets, after which he placed a muzzle of a pistol in the back of the robber's neck and sharply commanded:

"Hands up!"

Up went the robber's hands as if he were a jumping-jack jerked by a string, whereupon his late victim, doubtless animated by the same emotions as those of the other citizens, fled away like the wind, but not in silence, for at every jump he bellowed, "Thieves, murder, help!"

A window slammed up in the house before which they were standing and the glare of an electric bicycle lamp played full upon Mr. Middleton and his prisoner.

"I've got him," said Mr. Middleton, proudly.

"Got him! Got him!" gasped an astonished voice. "Well, of all effrontery! Got him, you miserable thief? The police are coming and they'll get you, and I can identify you, if they don't succeed in nabbing you red-handed."

Shocked and almost paralyzed, Mr. Middleton turned to expostulate with the misled householder, when the robber, seizing the opportunity, fled away like the wind, bellowing at every jump, "Thieves, murder, help!" and as if aroused by the sound of his compatriot's voice, the thief who had been lying unconscious in the street all this while, arose and hastened away, somewhat unsteadily, it is true, yet at a considerable degree of speed.

It did not require any extended reflective processes for Mr. Middleton to tell himself that if he waited for the police, he would be in a very bad plight, for he had the stolen property upon his person, the thieves had gone, and even if the victims were able to say he was not one of the two original thieves—which their disturbed state of mind made most uncertain—they would be likely to declare him a thief notwithstanding, a charge which the stolen property on his person would bear out. The police could now be heard down the street and the householder was making the welkin ring with vociferous shouts. With a sudden access of rage at this individual whose well-intended efforts had thwarted justice and might yet fasten crime upon innocence, Mr. Middleton pointed a pistol at the upper pane of the window where shone the bicycle lamp. There was a roar that shook the air, followed by a crash of glass and the clatter of a dozen bullets upon the brick wall of the house, and a shriek of terror from the householder and the bicycle lamp instantly vanished. With a heart strangely at peace in the midst of the dangers that encompassed him, Mr. Middleton sped up the street, dashed through an alleyway, back for a block on the next street in the direction he had just come, and thenceforth leisurely and with an appearance of virtue he did not need to feign, made his way home without molestation.

Upon examining the booty that had so strangely come into his possession, Mr. Middleton was at a loss to think which were the greater villains, those who had robbed, or those who had been robbed. One wallet contained five hundred and forty dollars in greenbacks and some memoranda accompanying it showed that it was a corruption fund to be used in bribing voters at an approaching election. The other wallet contained sixty dollars and a detailed plan for bribery, fraud, and intimidation which was to be carried out in one of the doubtful wards. There were also some silver coins, and two gold watches bearing no names or marks that could identify their owners, but the detailed plan contained the name of the politician who had drawn it up and who was to be benefited by its successful accomplishment. This was a clue by following which Mr. Middleton might have found the parties who had been robbed and return their property, but he was deterred from doing so by several considerations. The knowledge he had of the proposed fraud was exceedingly dangerous to the interests of one of the political parties and to the personal interests of one of the bosses of that party. It would be clearly to their advantage to have Mr. Middleton jailed and so put where there would be no danger that he would divulge the information in his possession. Besides this, the money was to be used for corrupt purposes, would go into the hands of evil men who would spend it evilly. Deprived of it, a thoroughly bad man was less likely to be elected. For these moral and prudential reasons, Mr. Middleton saw that it was plainly his duty to the public and to himself to retain the money. The victims, bearing in mind that the recovery of the money by the police would also mean the discovery of the incriminating documents and that any persecution of the robbers might incite them to sell the documents to the opposite party, would be very chary about doing or saying anything. But there was the householder, who surely would tell his tale and who had an idea of Mr. Middleton's personal appearance. Accordingly, that excellent young man disposed of the gold watches to one Isaac Fiscovitz on lower State Street, and with the results of the exchange purchased an entirely new suit, new hat, and new shoes. The incriminating documents, he placed under the carpet in his room against a time when he might see an opportunity to safely dispose of them to the pecuniary advantage of himself and to the discomfiture of the contemptible creature whose handiwork they were.

He said nothing of these transactions when on the appointed evening he once more sat in the presence of the urbane prince of the tribe of Al-Yam. Having handed him a bowl of delicately flavored sherbet, Achmed began the narration of The Adventure of Miss Clarissa Dawson.

THE ADVENTURE OF MISS CLARISSA DAWSON.

MISS CLARISSA DAWSON was a young lady who had charge of the cutlery counter in one of the great emporiums of State Street. She was reckoned of a pretty wit and not more cutting were the Sheffield razors that were piled before her than the remarks she sometimes made to those who, incited thereto by her reputation for readiness of retort, sought to engage her in a contest of repartee. It was seldom that she issued from these encounters other than triumphant, leaving her presumptuous opponents defeated and chagrined. But in the month of November of the last year, for once she owned to herself that she had been overcome,—overcome, it is true, because her adversary was plainly a person of stupidity, mailed by his doltishness against the keenest sarcasm she could launch against him, yet nevertheless overcome. To her choicest bit of irony, the individual replied, "Somebody left you on the grindstone and forgot to take you off," to which the most adroit in quips and quirks could find no fitting replication, unless it were to indulge in facial contortion or invective, and Miss Clarissa was too much of a lady to do either. Forced into silence, she had no resource but to seek to transfix him with a protracted and contemptuous stare, which, though failing to disconcert the object, put her in possession of the facts that he had mild blue eyes, that the remnants of his hair were red, that he was slightly above middle height and below middle age, and that there was little about his face and still less his figure to distinguish him from a multitude of men of the average type. Indeed, one could not even conjecture his nationality, for his type was one to be seen in all branches of the Indo-European race. If from a package in his upper left-hand coat pocket, which, broken, disclosed some wieners, you concluded he was of the German nation, a short dudeen in an upper vest pocket would seem to indicate that he was an Irishman. His coat was of black cheviot, new, and of the current cut. His vest was of corduroy, of the kind in vogue in the past decade, while his pantaloons, black, with a faint green line in them, were a compromise, being of a non-commital cut that would never be badly out of style in any modern period.

Sustaining Miss Clarissa's stare with great composure, he purchased six German razors at thirty-five cents each, six English at fifty, twelve American at the same price, and a stray French razor at sixty-two.

"Don't you want some razorine?" asked Miss Clarissa. "It makes razors—and other things—sharper."

"Why don't you use it, then, instead of lobsterine?" replied the stranger, picking up his package and the change. Miss Clarissa deigning to give no reply but an angry frown, the stranger expressed his gratitude for the amusement he intimated she had afforded him and he further said he hoped he would see her at the Charity Ball and he made bold to ask her to save the second two-step for him, and thereafter departed, having declined Miss Clarissa's offer to have his purchases sent to his address, an offer dictated not by a spirit of accommodation and kindliness, but by a desire to learn in what part of the city he had his residence.

On the morrow again came a man to purchase razors, of which there was a large number on Miss Clarissa's counter, traveling men's samples for sale at ridiculous prices. The man had purchased two dozen razors before Miss Clarissa, noting this similarity to the transactions of the odious person and thereby led to take a good look at him, observed with astonishment that this new man had on exactly the same suit that had been worn by the purchaser of the day before. She recognized the fabric, the color, everything down to a discoloration on the left coat lapel. Here the resemblance ended. The second individual was a young man. He had a heavy shock of abundant hair. He was not more than twenty-eight years old and so far from being commonplace, he was of a distinguished appearance. But as the eyes of Miss Clarissa continued to dwell upon him in some admiration, she told herself that the resemblance did not end with the clothes, after all. His eyes were of the same blue, his hair of the same auburn as those of the man of yesterday. Indeed, the man of yesterday might have been this man with twenty years added on him, with the light of hope and ambition dimmed by contact with the world, and his youthful alertness and dash succeeded by the resigned vacuity of one who has seen none of his early dreams realized. Again did Miss Clarissa ask if he would have his purchases sent to his address, but this time it was not entirely curiosity and the perfunctory performance of a duty, for she would gladly have been of service to one of such a pleasing presence. Communing with himself for a moment, the young man said:

"On the whole, you may. But they must be delivered to me in person, into my own hands. I would take them, but I have a number of other things to take. Remember, they are to be delivered to me in person," and he handed her a card which announced that his name was Asbury Fuller and on which was written in lead pencil the address of a house in a quarter of the city which, once the most fashionable of all, had suffered from the encroachments of trade and where a few mansions yet occupied by the aristocracy were surrounded by the deserted homes of families which had fled to the newer haunts of fashion, leaving their former abodes to be occupied by boarding mistresses, dentists, doctors, clairvoyants, and a whole host of folk whose names would never be in the papers until their burial permits were issued.

Miss Clarissa did a very peculiar thing. It was already four o'clock of a Saturday afternoon. Instead of immediately giving the package into the hands of the delivery department, she retained it and, at closing time, going to the room where ready made uniforms for messenger boys were kept, she purloined one. Now it must be known that the principal reason for doing a thing so unusual, not to say indiscreet, was her desire to obey the young man's injunction to hand the razors into his own hands and no others. She had become possessed of the idea that some disaster would befall if the razors came into the possession of any one else. Moreover, the stranger had humbled her in the contest of repartee, which, as a true woman, had made her entertain an admiration for him, and this and his strange disguises and his unaccountable purchases had surrounded him with a mist of romantic mystery she fain would penetrate. Some little time before, it had been Miss Clarissa's misfortune, through sickness, to lose much of her hair. It had now begun to grow again and resume its former luxuriant abundance, but by removing several switches—of her own hair—and the bolster commonly called a rat, and sleeking her hair down hard with oil, she appeared as a boy might who was badly in need of a haircut. After a light supper, she set out alone for the residence of Asbury Fuller and at the end of her journey found herself at the gateway of a somber edifice, which was apparently the only one in the block that was inhabited. On either side and across the way were vacant houses, lonesome and forbidding. Indeed, the residence of Asbury Fuller was itself scarcely less lonesome and forbidding. The grass of the plot before it was long and unkempt and heavily covered with mats of autumn leaves. The bricks of the front walk were sunken and uneven and the steps leading to the high piazza were deeply warped, as by pools of water that had lain and dried on their unswept surface through many seasons. The blinds hung awry and the paint on the great front doors was scaling, and altogether it was a faded magnificence, this of Asbury Fuller. She pulled the handle of the front-door bell and in response to its jangling announcement came a maid.

"Asbury Fuller?" said the maid, omitting the "Mr." Miss Clarissa had affixed. "Go to the side door around to the right."

Wondering if this were a lodging house and Asbury Fuller had a private entrance, or if it being his own house he had left word that callers should be sent to the side door to prevent the delivery of the razors being seen by others, Clarissa followed the walk through an avenue of dead syringa bushes and came to the side door. The same maid who had met her before, ushered her in and presently she found herself in a small apartment, almost a closet, standing at the back of Asbury Fuller. But though small, she remarked that the apartment was one of some magnificence, for on all sides was a quantity of burnished copper, binding the edges of a row of shelves and covering the whole top of a broad counter-like projection running along one side of the wall. Before this, Asbury Fuller was standing, assorting a number of cut-glass goblets of various sizes and putting them upon silver salvers, bottles of various colored wines being placed upon each salver with the goblets. He turned at her entrance and the look of sad and gloomy abstraction sitting upon his countenance instantly changed to one of relief and joy.

"At last, at last," he exclaimed, in a deep tone which even more than his countenance betrayed his relief and joy. "It is almost too late and I thought the young woman had not attended to sending them, that she had failed me."

"She would not fail you, sir," said Clarissa, earnestly, allowing herself in the protection her assumed character gave her the pleasure of giving utterance to her feeling of regard for the young man. "She would not fail, sir, she could not fail you. Oh, you wrong her, if you think she could ever break her word to you."

Asbury Fuller bent an inscrutable look upon Clarissa and then bidding her remain until his return, hastily left the room. But though he was gone, Clarissa sat gloating upon the mental picture of his manly beauty. He seemed taller than before, for the stoop he had worn in the afternoon had now departed and he stood erect and muscular in the suit of full evening dress that set off his lithe, soldierly form to such advantage. His garb was of an elegance such as Clarissa had never before beheld, and it was plain that the aristocracy affected certain adornments in the privacy of their homes which they did not caparison themselves with in public. Clarissa had seen dress suits in restaurants and in theaters, but never before had she seen a bottle-green dress coat with gold buttons and a velvet collar and a vest with broad longitudinal stripes of white and brown. In a brief space, Asbury Fuller returned, and glancing at his watch, he said:

"There is some time before the dinner party begins and I would like to talk with you. I am impressed by your apparent honesty and particularly by the air of devotion to duty that characterizes you. The latter I have more often remarked in women than in the more selfish sex to which we belong. We need a boy here. Wages, twenty dollars a month and keep."

"Oh, sir, I should be pleased to come."

"Your duties will commence at once. Owing to the fact that this old house has been empty for some time and the work of rehabilitating and refurnishing it is far from completed, you cannot at present have a room to yourself. You will sleep with John Klussmann, the hostler——"

"Oh, sir, I cannot do that," exclaimed Clarissa, starting up in alarm.

"John is a good boy and kicks very little in his sleep. But doubtless you object to the smell of horses."

"Oh, sir, let me do what is needed this evening and go home and I will come back and work to-morrow and go home to-morrow night, and if by that time you find I can have a room by myself, perhaps I will come permanently."

"I don't smell of horses myself," said Asbury Fuller, musingly, to which Clarissa making no response other than turning away her head to hide her blushes, he continued. "But two days will be enough. Indeed, to-night is the crucial point. I will not beat about the bush longer. I wish to attach you to my interests. I wish you to serve me to-night in the crisis of my career."

"Oh, sir," said Clarissa, in the protection that her assumed character gave her, allowing herself the privilege of speaking her real sentiments, "I am attached to your interests. Let me serve you. Command, and I will use my utmost endeavor to obey."

Asbury Fuller looked at her in surprise. Carried away by her feelings and in the state of mental exaltation which the romance and mystery of the adventure had induced, she had made a half movement to kneel as she thus almost swore her fealty in solemn tones.

"Why are you attached to my interests?" asked Asbury Fuller, somewhat dryly.

Alas, Clarissa could not take advantage of the protection her assumed character gave her to tell the real reason. Only as a woman could she do that, only as a woman could she say and be believed, "Because I love you."

"Why, some people are naturally leaders, naturally draw others to them——"

"You cannot be a spy upon me, since no one knows who I am."

"A spy!" cried Clarissa, in a voice whose sorrowful reproach gave convincing evidence of her ingenuousness.

"I wrong you, I wrong you," said Asbury Fuller. "I will trust you. I will tell you what you are to do——"

"Butler," said a maid, poking her head in at the door, "it is time to come and give the finishing touches to the table. It is almost time for the dinner to be served," and without ado, Asbury Fuller sprang out of the room.

A butler! A butler! Clarissa sat stunned. It was thus that her hero had turned out. Could she tell the other girls in the store with any degree of pride that she was keeping company with a butler? She had received a good literary education in the high school at Muncie, Indiana, and was a young woman of taste and refinement. Could she marry a butler? To be near her hero, she herself had just now been willing to undertake a menial position. But she had then imagined him to be a person of importance. This stage in her cogitations led her to the reflection that her feelings were unworthy of her. Had her regard for Asbury Fuller been all due to the belief that he was a person of importance, merely the worship of position, the selfish desire and hope—however faint—of rising to affluence and social dignity through him? Butler or no butler, Asbury Fuller was handsome, he was distinguished, his manner of speech was superior to that of any person she had ever known. Butler or no butler, she loved him. Just now she had hoped that he, rich and well placed, would overlook her poverty, and take her, friendless and obscure, for his bride. Could she give less than she had hoped he would give? And then as butler, her chances of winning him were so greatly increased.

In a short time, he returned. He told her she was to wait on the table and instructed her how to serve the courses.

"The master will look surprised when he sees you instead of me. If he asks who you are, say the new page. But he will be too much afraid of exciting the wonder of his guests to ask you any questions. I feel certain that he will accept your presence without question, being desirous his guests shall not think him a tyro in the management of an establishment like this. I feel certain that after dinner, his guests will ask to see his collection of arms. Indeed, Miss Bording told him in my hearing last Monday that she accepted his invitation here on condition that she be allowed to see the famous collection. You are to follow them into the drawing-room after dinner. The master will not know whether that is usual or not. If they do start to go to look at the arms, you are to say, 'The collection of your former weapons, sir, has been placed in the first room to the left at the head of the stairs. The paper-hangers and decorators have been busy.' Then you are to lead the way into that room, which you will find dimly lighted. After that, I will attend to everything myself."

Although Clarissa could not but wonder at the strangeness of her instructions and to be somewhat alarmed at the evidences of a plot in which she was to be an agent, she agreed, for though her regard for Asbury Fuller would have been sufficient to cause such acquiescence, so great was her curiosity to have solved the mysteries which surrounded that individual, that this alone would have gained her consent.

There were but two guests at the table of Mr. William Leadbury—Judge Volney Bording, and his daughter, Eulalia Bording. Mr. Leadbury cast a look of surprise and displeasure as he saw Clarissa serving the first course, but he quickly concealed these emotions and proceeded to plunge into an animated conversation with his guests. Indeed, it assumed the character of a monologue in which he frequently adverted to the weather, to be off on a tangent the next moment on a discussion of finance, politics, sociology, on which subjects, however, he was far from showing the positiveness and fixed opinion that he did while descanting upon the weather. In all the subjects he touched upon, he exhibited a certain skill in so framing his remarks that they would not run counter to any prejudices or opposite opinions of his auditors, but the feelings of the auditors having been elicited, served as a preamble from which he could go on, warmly agreeing with their views in the further and more complete unfolding of his own. He was between twenty-seven and thirty years of age, of a somewhat spare figure, and in the well-proportioned features of his face there was no one that would attract attention beyond the others and easily remain fixed in memory. He was not without an appearance of intelligence and his chest was thrown out and the small of his back drawn in after the manner of the Prussian ex-sergeants who give instruction in athletics and the cultivation of a proper carriage to the elite of this city, and withal he had the appearance of a person of substance and of consequence in his community. In the midst of a pause where he was occupied in putting his soup-spoon into his mouth, Miss Bording remarked:

"Please do not talk about commonplace American subjects, Mr. Leadbury. Tell us of your foreign life. Tell us of Algeria. What sort of a country is Algeria?"

Turning his eyes toward the chandelier about him and with an elegance of enunciation that did much to relieve the undeniably monotonous evenness of his discourse, he began:

"Algeria, the largest and most important of the French colonial possessions, is a country of northern Africa, bounded on the north by the Mediterranean, west by Morocco, south by the desert of Sahara, and east by Tunis. It extends for about five hundred and fifty miles along the coast and inland from three hundred to four hundred miles. Physiographically it may be roughly divided into three zones," and so on for a considerable length until by an accident which Clarissa could attribute to nothing but inconceivable awkwardness, Judge Bording dropped a glass of water, crash! Having ceased his disquisition at this accident, so disconcerting to the judge, Miss Bording very prettily and promptly thanked him for his information and saying that she now had a clear understanding of the principal facts pertaining to Algeria, abruptly changed the subject by asking him if he had heard anything more concerning his second cousin, the barber.

"There is nothing more to be heard. He is dead. You know he came here about a week before I did. By the terms of my uncle's will, the five years to be allowed to elapse before I was to be considered dead or disappeared would have come to an end in a week after the time of my arrival, and the property have passed to him, my uncle's cousin. By the greatest luck in the world, I had become homesick and throwing up my commission in the Foreign Legion, or Battalion D'Etranger, as we have it in French, which is, as you may know, a corps of foreigners serving under the French flag, mainly in Algeria, but occasionally in other French possessions—throwing up my commission, I came home, bringing with me my famous collection of weapons and the fauteuil of Ab del Kader, the armchair, you understand, of the great Arab prince who led the last revolt against France. It was not all homesickness, either. Among the men of all nationalities serving in the Foreign Legion, are many adventurous Americans, and a young Chicagoan, remarking my name, apprised me of the fact that perhaps I was heir to a fortune in Chicago. I came," continued Leadbury, looking down toward his lap, where Clarissa saw he held a clipping from a newspaper, "and took apartments at the Bennington Hotel, where, when seen by the representatives of the 'Commercial Advertiser,' the following interesting facts were brought out in the interview: 'William Leadbury'—your humble servant—" he interjected, "'is the only son of the late Charles Leadbury, only brother of the late millionaire iron merchant, James Leadbury. Upon his death, James Leadbury left his entire property'—but," said Leadbury, looking up, "I have previously covered that point."

"But tell us of your weapons," interposed Miss Bording.

"Oh, yes, that seems to interest you," and deftly sliding the clipping along in his fingers, he resumed: "'The collection of weapons is one of the most interesting and remarkable collections in the United States, for, though not large, its owner can say, with pardonable pride, "every bit of steel in that collection has been used by me in my trade."'"

"Ah, how proud you must be," mused Miss Bording. "I read something like that in the papers, myself. Just to think of it! Every bit of steel in that collection has been used by you in your trade. What a strange affectation you military men have in calling your profession a trade! But, Captain Leadbury, tell me of your cousin, who disappeared two days after your arrival, and why you shaved your moustache which the papers described you as having."

"A moustache is a bother," said Leadbury. "As to my cousin, why, overcome by disappointment, he took to drink. He disappeared from his lodgings on Rush Street two days after my arrival, at the close of a twenty-four hours' debauch. It was found he had shipped as a sailor on the Ingar Gulbrandson, lumber hooker for Marinette, and the Gulbrandson was found sunk up by Death's Door, at the entrance to Green Bay, her masts sticking above water. Her crew had utterly disappeared. That was three months ago and neither hide nor hair of any of them has been seen since. Poor Anderson Walkley is dead! Were he alive, I would be glad to assist him. But he was a rover, never long in one place—a few months here, a few months there—and now he is at rest and I believe he is glad, I believe he is glad."

The second course consisted of turkey, and Clarissa was astounded, as she deposited the dishes of the course, to see Asbury Fuller swiftly enter the door upon all-fours and with extreme celerity and cat-like lightness, flit across the room and esconce himself behind a huge armchair upholstered in velvet, and her astonishment increased and was tinged with no small degree of terror, as she observed the chair, noiselessly and almost imperceptibly, progress across the floor, propelled by some hidden force, until it reached a station behind the master of the house. Captain Leadbury began to carve the turkey and Clarissa was astonished more than ever to hear, in the Captain's voice, though she was sure his lips were shut,

"Would you like a close shave, Miss Bording?"

The sound of the carving-knife dropping upon the platter as Leadbury started in some sudden spasm of pain, was drowned by the silvery laughter of Miss Bording, saying,

"Oh, don't make fun of the profession of your poor cousin, Captain," and the look of disquiet upon Leadbury's face was quickly relieved and he joined heartily and almost boisterously in the merriment. A moment later, Clarissa was alarmed to find him bending upon herself a look in which suspicion, distrust, fear, and hatred all were blended.

Judge Volney Bording, ornament to the legal profession, was a hearty eater, and it was not long before he sent his plate for a second helping, and again Clarissa heard from the closed lips of Leadbury, in a voice that seemed to float up from his very feet:

"Next. Next. You're next, Miss Bording. What'll it be?"

Leadbury half rose, looking toward Clarissa with a glance of most violent anger, but whatever he would have said, was again interrupted by the silvery laugh of Miss Bording, and again Leadbury joined heartily, almost boisterously. But though he regained his self-possession and his brow became serene, Clarissa saw in his eye that which told he had a reckoning in store for her when once the guests were out of the house, but that in the meantime he would dissemble the various unpleasant emotions with which his mind was filled. The rest of the dinner passed without untoward event. The huge armchair by imperceptible degrees retired to its former position, and as Clarissa set down the dessert, she saw Asbury Fuller, with a grace unusual and not to be expected of one in such a posture, proceeding quickly and silently out of the room upon all-fours.

Mindful of her instructions, Clarissa accompanied the party when, rising from the table, they withdrew to the drawing-room. It was manifest that her presence caused Leadbury some uneasiness and he looked now at her and now at his guests with an inquiring and perturbed countenance, but in the calm faces of the judge and his daughter he could detect nothing to indicate that they thought the presence of the page at all strange, and little by little he recovered his good spirits and related some interesting anecdotes of a bulldog he once owned and of a colored person who stole a guitar from him. But though Miss Bording gave a courteous and interested attention and laughed at the anecdotes of the dog, she irked at the necessity of silence, which the garrulity of her host placed her under and was desirous of having the conversation become general and of a more entertaining, elevated and instructive character. As the narration of the episode of the colored person came to an end, she hastily exclaimed:

"Captain, you promised to show us your collection. It is nearing the time when we must go home, for father has had to-day to listen to an unparalleled amount of gabble and is very tired."

"I will show the collection to you with great pleasure," said Leadbury, and at this juncture, Clarissa, remembering her instructions, said:

"The collection of your former weapons, sir, has been placed in the first room at the left at the head of the stairs. The paperhangers and decorators have been busy." And then she proceeded to lead the way into the hall and up the broad funereal staircase that led above. Dimly burned the lights in the hall. Dimly burned a gas jet in the room whose door stood open at the left.

"Oh, yes," said Leadbury, gaily, responding to a remark of Miss Bording, as they entered the room and saw the uncertain shape of a large chair vaguely looming in the gloom; "I secured the fauteuil of Ab del Kader after we had stormed the last stronghold of that unfortunate prince. But interesting as this relic is, I put no value upon it in comparison with the weapons, for every bit of steel in the collection has been used by me in my trade."

As he said these words, he turned on the gas at full head and the light blazed forth to be shot back from an array of polished steel festooned upon the wall, a glittering rosette, but not of sabres and scimetars, yataghans, rapiers, broadswords, dirks and poniards, pistols, fusils and rifles. No! Razors and scissors! Before this array sat a great red velvet barber's chair, and near them on the wall was a board, bearing little brass hooks, upon each of which hung a green ticket.

In the unexpected revelation that had followed the flare of light, all eyes were turned upon William Leadbury, swaying back and forward with one hand clinging to the big chair, as if ready to swoon. A sickly, cringing grin played over his face, suddenly come all a-yellow, and his long tongue was flickering over his pale lips. But all at once his muscles sprang tense and a malignant anger tightened his quivering features and turning upon Clarissa, he hissed:

"You did this. You exposed me, you exposed me," and he was about to leap at the terrified girl, when a ringing voice cried, "Stop!" and there was Asbury Fuller standing in the doorway with the broad red cordon of a Commander of the Legion of Honor across his breast and a glittering rapier in his hand. Clarissa could have fallen at his feet, he looked so handsome and grand, and she could have scratched out the eyes of Eulalia Bording, whose gaze betrayed an admiration equal to her own. Asbury Fuller, yet not wearing quite his wonted appearance, for the luxuriant locks of auburn had gone and his head was covered with a short, though thick crop of chestnut.

"You exposed yourself. Harmless would all this have been, powerless to hurt you, if you had kept your self-possession and turned it off as a joke— your own. But your abashed mien, your complete confusion, your utter disconcertment, betrayed you, even if you had no longer left any question by crying out that you have been exposed. Yes, exposed, Anderson Walkley, by the sudden confronting of you with the implements of your craft, the weapons you had used in your trade, and the belief thus aroused in your guilty mind that your secret was known, that your identity had been detected."

"Asbury Fuller, what business is it of yours?" and Leadbury snatched up a large pair of hair clippers and waved them with a menacing gesture.

"Everyman to the weapons of his trade," exclaimed Asbury Fuller, and the hair clippers seemed suddenly enveloped in a mass of white flame, as the rapier played about them. Cling, clang, across the room flew the clippers, twisted from Leadbury's hand as neatly as you please.

"Asbury Fuller?" cried the Commander of the Legion of Honor. "Asbury Fuller?" and he deftly fastened beneath his nose an elegant false moustache with waxed ends.

With his hands before his eyes as if to forefend his view from some dreadful apparition, the man in the corner sank upon his knees, gibbering, "William Leadbury, come back from the dead!"

"William Leadbury, alive and well, here to claim his own from you, Anderson Walkley, outlaw and felon. Your plans were well-laid, but I am not dead. You signed the papers of the Ingar Gulbrandson in your proper person. Then as she was about to sail, I was brought aboard ostensibly drunk, but really drugged, under the name of Anderson Walkley. The Gulbrandson was found sunk. Her crew of four had utterly disappeared. Dead, of course. The records gave their names. I had become Anderson Walkley and was dead. You had seized my property and my identity. I had been in Chicago but two days and no one had become familiar enough with my appearance to make any question when you with your clean-shaven face came down on the morning after my kidnaping and told the people at the hotel that you were William Leadbury and had shaved your moustache off over night. Whatever difference they might have thought they saw, was easily explained by the change occasioned by the removal of your moustache. Had your minions been as intelligent as they were villainous, your scheme would have succeeded. It was necessary to drug me anew on the voyage, as the effects were wearing off. They did not drug me enough, and when they scuttled the old hulk and rowed ashore to flee with their blood money, the cold water rising in the sinking vessel awoke me, brought me to full consciousness, and I easily got ashore on some planking. I saw at once what the plot had been. I realized I had a desperate man to deal with. I had no money and it would take me some time to get from northern Wisconsin to Chicago. In the meantime, every one would have come to believe you William Leadbury, and who would believe me, the ragged tramp, suddenly appearing from nowhere and claiming to be the heir? You would be coached by your lawyers, have time to concoct lies, to manufacture conditions that would color your claim, and in court you would be self-possessed and on your guard. Therefore I felt that I must await the psychological moment when you could be taken off your guard, when, surprised and in confusion, you would betray yourself. I secured employment as your butler, the psychological moment came, and you stand, self-convicted, thief and would-be murderer."

"Send for the police at once," said Judge Bording.

"No," said the late captain in the Foreign Legion. "He may reform. I wish him to have another chance. That he may have the wherewithal to earn a livelihood, I present him with the contents of this room, the means of his undoing. In my uncle's library are many excellent theological works of a controversial nature, and these, too, I present to him, as a means of turning his thoughts toward better things. I will not send for the police. I will send for a dray. Judge Bording, by the recent concatenation of events, I am become the host. Let us leave Walkley here to pack his effects, and return to the drawing-room."

Clarissa preceded the others as they slowly descended, with all her ears open to hear whatsoever William Leadbury might say to Eulalia Bording, and it was so that she noted a strange little creaking above them, and looking up, saw poised upon the edge of the balustrade in the upper hall, impending over the head of William Leadbury and ready to fall, the great barber chair! With a swift leap, she pushed him to the wall, causing him to just escape the chair as it fell with a dreadful crash. But she herself was not so fortunate, for with a wicked tunk the cushioned back of the chair struck her a glancing blow that felled her senseless upon the stairs.

Judge Bording flew after the dastardly barber, who swifter still, was down the backstairs and out of the house into the darkness before the Judge could lay hands upon him.

The judge, his daughter, and William Leadbury, bent over the unconscious form of the page.

"He saved your life," said the judge. "The wood and iron part would have hit your head."

"His breath is knocked out of him," said Miss Bording.

"He saved my life. I cannot understand his strange devotion. I cannot understand it," said William Leadbury, the while opening the page's vest, tearing away his collar, and straining at his shirt, that the stunned lungs might have play and get to work again. The stiffly starched shirt resisted his efforts and he reached in under it to detach the fastenings of the studs that held the bosom together. Back came his hand as if it had encountered a serpent beneath that shirt front.

"I begin to understand," he exclaimed, and bending an enigmatical look upon the startled judge and his daughter, he picked the page up in his arms with the utmost tenderness, and bore him away.

The pains in Clarissa's body had left her. Indeed, they had all but gone when on Sunday morning, after a night which had been one of formless dreams where she had not known whether she slept or waked or where she was, a frowsy maid had called her from the bed where she lay beneath a blanket, fully dressed, and told her it was time she was getting back to the city. Not a sign of William Leadbury as she passed out of the great silent house. Not a word from him, no inquiry for the welfare of the little page who had come so nigh dying for him. Clarissa was too proud to do or say anything to let the frowsy maid guess that she wondered at this or cared aught for the ungrateful captain. She steeled her heart against him, but though as the days went by she succeeded in ceasing to care for one who was so unworthy of her regard, she could not stifle the poignant regret that he was thus unworthy.

It had come Friday evening, almost closing time in the great store. Slowly and heavily, Clarissa was setting her counter in order, preparing to go to her lodgings and nurse her sick heart until slumber should give respite from her pain, when there came a messenger from the dress-making department asking her presence there.

"We've just got an order for a ready-made ball-dress for a lady that is unexpectedly going to the Charity Ball to-night," said Mrs. McGuffin, head of the department. "The message says the lady is just your height and build and color—she noticed you sometime, it seems—and that we are to fit one of the dresses to you, making such alterations as would make it fit you, choosing one suitable to your complexion. When it's done, to save time, you are to go right to the person who ordered it, without stopping to change your clothes. You can do that there. It will make her late to the ball, at best. A carriage and a person to conduct you will be waiting."

It was a magnificent dress that was gradually built upon the figure of Clarissa, and when at last it was completed and she stood before the great pier glass flushed with the radiance of a pleasure she could not but feel despite her late sorrow and the fact she was but the lay figure for a more fortunate woman, one would have to search far to find a more beautiful creature.

"Whyee!" exclaimed Mrs. McGuffin. "Why, I had no idea you had such a figure. Why, I must have you in my department to show off dresses on. You will work at the cutlery counter not a day after to-morrow. But there, I am keeping you. The ball must almost have begun. Here's a bag with your things in it. I was going to say, 'your other things.'" And throwing a splendid cloak about the lovely shoulders of Miss Clarissa, Mrs. McGuffin turned her over to the messenger.

There was already somebody in the carriage into which Clarissa stepped, but as the curtain was drawn across the opposite window, she was unable to even conjecture the sex of the individual who was to be her conductor to her destination, and steeped in dreams which from pleasant ones quickly passed to bitter, she speedily forgot all about the person at her side. But presently she perceived their carriage had come into the midst of a squadron of other carriages charging down upon a brilliantly lighted entrance where men and women, brave in evening dress, were moving in.

"Why, we are going to the ball-room itself," and as she said this and realized that here on the very threshold of the entrancing gayeties she was to put off her fine plumage and see the other woman pass out of the dressing-room into the delights beyond, while she crept away in her own simple garb amid the questioning, amused, and contemptuous stares of the haughty dames who had witnessed the exchange, she broke into a piteous sob.

"Why, of course to the ball-room, my darling," breathed a voice, which low though it was, thrilled her more than the voice of an archangel, and she felt herself strained to a man's heart and her bare shoulders, which peeped from the cloak at the thrust of a pair of strong arms beneath it, came in contact with the cool, smooth surface of the bosom of a dress shirt. "Don't you remember that I engaged the second two-step at the Charity Ball?"

Clarissa, almost swooning with joy as she reclined palpitating upon the manly breast of Captain William Leadbury, said never a word, for the power of speech was not in her; the power of song, of uttering peans of joy, perhaps, but not the power of speech.

"Have I assumed too much," said Leadbury, gravely, relaxing somewhat the tightness of his embrace. "Have I, arguing from the fact that you both served me in the crisis of my career and saved my life, assumed too much in believing you love me? If so, I beg your pardon for arranging this surprise. I will release you. I———"

"Oh, no," crooned Clarissa, nestling against him with all the quivering protest of a child about to be taken from its mother. "You read my actions rightly. Oh, how I have suffered this week. No word from you. I could not understand it. Of course you could not know I was a girl. But I thought you ought to be grateful, even to a boy."

"But I did know you were a girl. When you fell, I began to open the clothes about your chest. When I discovered your sex, I carried you upstairs, placed you on a bed, threw a blanket over you and was about to call Miss Bording to take charge of you———"

"I'm glad you didn't. I don't like Miss Bording," said Clarissa.

"I had left to call her, when that poltroon of an Anderson Walkley, who had stolen back into the house after running from it, crept behind me and struck me back of the ear with a shaving mug. I dropped unconscious. In the resulting confusion, your very existence was as forgotten as your whereabouts was unknown. You lay there as I had left you until a maid found you in the morning and packed you off. It was not until Wednesday that I was able to be out. I knew you came from this store, and mousing about in there, I had no trouble in identifying the nice young page with the beautiful young woman at the cutlery counter. I could scarce wait two days, but as three had already passed, I planned this surprise, remembering our banter when I talked with you, disguised as a man of fifty, and now you are to go in with me as my affianced bride. We'd better hurry, for the driver must be wondering what we are thinking about."

It was worthy of remark that even the ladies passed many compliments upon the beauty and grace of Miss Clarissa Dawson, the young woman who came to the ball with William Leadbury, former captain in the army of the Republique Française, heir to the millions of the late James Leadbury, and a number of persons esteemed judges of all that pertains to the Terpsichorean art, declared that when she appeared upon the floor for the first time, which was to dance the second two-step with the gallant soldier, that such was the surpassing grace with which she revolved over the floor that one might well say she seemed to be dancing upon air.

WHAT BEFELL MR. MIDDLETON BECAUSE OF THE SIXTH GIFT OF THE EMIR.

"IT IS strange," said Mr. Middleton, "that after Clarissa had shown her devotion to the extent of saving his life, Captain Leadbury could have had, even for a moment, any misgivings that she loved him."

"One cannot always be sure," said the emir. "A lover, being in a highly nervous state because of his emotion, is always more or less unstrung and unable to form a sound judgment or behave rationally. It is because of this, that there are so many lovers' quarrels. But one need not be at sea as regards the question of the affection of the object of his tender passion. It is only necessary for you to wear a philter upon the forehead and you can obtain the love of any woman," and giving Mesrour some directions, the Nubian brought to his master a minute bag of silk an inch square and of wafer thinness, which, both from its appearance and the rare odor of musk which it exhaled, resembled a sachet bag.

"Wear this on your forehead," said the emir, presenting it to Mr. Middleton.

"But I would look ridiculous doing that, and excite comment," expostulated the student of law.

"Not at all," said the emir. "Put it inside the sweat-band of the front of your hat and no one will perceive it and yet it will have all its potency."

Which, accordingly, Mr. Middleton did, and having thanked the emir for his entertainment and instruction and the gift, he departed.

The close of the relation of the adventure of Miss Clarissa Dawson left Mr. Middleton in a most amorous mood. His mind was full of soft dreams of the delight William Leadbury must have experienced as he sat in the hack with Clarissa's cheek against his, pouring forth his love into her surprised ear. Before retiring for the night, he sat for some time ciphering on the back of an envelope and kept putting down "$1,000, $500, $560; $560, $500, $1,000; $500, $560, $1,000; $500, $1,000, $560," but as the result of the addition was never over $2,060, whatever way he put it, and as the stipend he received for his labors in the law offices of Brockelsby and Brockman was but $26 a month, he did not feel that he had any business to snatch the young lady of Englewood to his breast and tell her of his love and his bank account.

He went to see her on the following night. The exquisite beauty of this peerless young woman had never so impressed him as upon this night and he was gnawed by the most intense longing to call her his own. As he thought of the fortunate William Leadbury with his rich uncle, he fairly hated him, and anon he cursed Brockelsby and Brockman for refusing to raise his salary to a point commensurate with the value of his services. Surely, the young lady of Englewood, even were he to believe her gifted with only ordinary penetration, instead of being the highly intelligent and perspicacious person he knew her to be, could see how he felt and must know that it was only a question of time and more money, and assuredly, one so gracious could not, in view of the circumstances, begrudge him the advance of one kiss and one embrace pending the formal offer of himself and his fortunes. So as he stood in the doorway, bidding her good-night, right in the midst of an irrelevant remark concerning the weather, he suddenly and without warning, threw his arms about her and essayed to kiss her. But the young lady of Englewood, with a cry commingled of surprise and horror, sprang away.

"How dare you sir? What made you do that? What sort of a girl do you think I am?" she said in freezing tones.

Mr. Middleton replied, stuttering weakly in a very husky voice, "I think you are a nice girl."

"A nice girl!" quoth the young lady of Englewood fiercely. "You know no nice girl would allow it. Nice girl, indeed. You think so. You know no nice girl would let you do such a thing," and she slammed the door in his face.

Away went Mr. Middleton with his heart full of bitterness because she would not let him do such a thing, and in the hallway stood the young lady of Englewood with her heart full of bitterness because he had tried to do such a thing and because she could not let him do such a thing.

"Much good was the philter," said Mr. Middleton, remembering the emir's gift, but almost at the same time, he recalled that the philter had not been on his forehead when he attempted to embrace the young lady of Englewood, for he had held his hat in his hand.

The farther he departed from her, the more his resentment grew, and he declared to himself that he would never have anything more to do with her. She was ungrateful, cold, haughty, not at all the kind of girl he could wish as his partner for life. He would proceed to let her see that he could do without her. He would cast her image from the temple of his heart and never go near her again. For a moment, he was disturbed by the thought that perhaps she would decline to receive him, even if he should call, but he quickly banished this unpleasant reflection and fell to devising means by which he might make it clearly apparent to the young lady of Englewood that he did not care.

"I'll make her sorry. I'll show her I don't care, I'll show her I don't care."

There is a restaurant under the basement of one of the larger and more celebrated saloons of the city, where a genial Gaul provides, for the modest sum of fifty cents, a course dinner, with wine. The wine is but ordinary California claret, but the viands are excellently cooked and of themselves sufficient inducement for a wight to part with half a dollar without consideration of the wine. There are those who, in the melancholy state that follows a disappointment in love, go without food and drink, while others turn to undue indulgence in drink. There are yet others, though few observers seem to have noted them, who turn toward greater indulgence in food, seeking surcease and forgetfulness of the pains of the heart in benefactions to the stomach.

It was very seldom that Mr. Middleton spent so much as fifty cents upon a meal, but the conduct of the young lady of Englewood having deprived him of any present object for laying up money, and, moreover, the pains of the heart before alluded to demanding the vicarious offices of the stomach, he went to the little French restaurant the next evening.

It was somewhat late when he arrived and there were in the room but two diners beside himself. These were a man and a woman, who by many little obvious evidences made manifest that they were not husband and wife. They had arrived at the dessert and were eating ice cream with genteel slowness, conversing the while with great decorum. Both were tall and fair, singularly well matched as to height and the ample and shapely proportions of their figures, and both were well, though quietly and even simply, dressed. They were nearly of an age, too, he being apparently forty, and she thirty-five. Their years sat lightly upon them, however, and if upon her face there were traces left by the longing for the lover who had not yet come into her life, that was all which upon either countenance betrayed that their lives had been other than care-free and happy. Assuredly, any one would have called them a fine looking man and woman. All this Mr. Middleton observed in a glance or two and then addressed himself to the comestibles that were set before him and doubtless would not have given the couple thought again, had not the waitress at the close of the meal fluttered at his elbows, placing the vinegar cruet and Worcestershire sauce bottle within easy reach, which services caused Mr. Middleton to look up in some wonder, as he was engaged with custard pie and he had never heard of any race of men, however savage, who used vinegar and Worcestershire sauce upon custard pie. The waitress, who was a young woman of a pleasant and intelligent countenance, met this glance with another compounded of mystery and communicativeness, and bending low while she removed the vinegar and Worcestershire sauce to a new station, murmured:

"That man over there has been here seven nights running, with a different woman every time."

Mr. Middleton sitting quiet in the surprise this information caused him, she repeated what she had said, adding, "and once he was here at noon besides, different woman every time."

Eight women in seven days! Certainly this was quite a curious thing.

"Do you know who he is? Have you ever seen any of the women before?"

"Nop. Don't know anything about him except what I have seen of him here. Never saw any of the women before—nor since."

Nor since. Mr. Middleton found himself asking himself if anybody had seen any of the women since. Had the girl in this chance remark unwittingly hit upon a terrible mystery? Nor since, nor since.

The man who had so suddenly assumed an interest in Mr. Middleton's eyes, arose, and going to the window, looked out at the street above, which was spattered with a sudden shower. He began to lament that he had not brought an umbrella and said he would go after one, when the storm so increased in violence that even a person provided with an umbrella—as was Mr. Middleton—would not care to venture into it, for such was the might of the wind now filling the air with its shrieks, that the rain swept in great lateral sheets which made an umbrella a futile protection. Yet notwithstanding this fury of the elements, the man of many women went out.

A half hour went by. An hour, and the storm did not abate and the man did not return. The good-looking waitress invited Mr. Middleton to sit at ease by a table in a rear part of the room, where lolling on the opposite side, with charming unconsciousness she let her hand lie stretched more than half across the board, a rampart of crumpled newspapers concealing it from the view of the eighth guest of the mulierose man. But whatever Mr. Middleton had done on previous occasions and might do on occasions yet to come, he now wished to avoid all appearances that might cause the eighth woman to regard him as at all inclined to other than discreet and modest conduct, for he was resolved to find out what he could about the man and eight women. So affecting not to note the hand temptingly disposed, he discoursed in a voice which was plainly audible in every corner of the room, not so much because of its loudness—for he had but little raised it—as because of a distinct and precise enunciation. This very precision, which always implies a regard for the rules, proprieties and amenities of life, seemed to stamp him as a man worthy of confidence, even had not his sentiments been of the most high-minded character. He described the great flood of 1882, which wrought such havoc in Missouri, in which cataclysm his Uncle Henry Perkins had suffered great loss. He extolled the commendable conduct of his uncle in sacrificing valuable property that he might save a woman; letting a flatboat loaded with twenty-five hogs whirl away in the raging flood, in order to rescue a woman from Booneville, Missouri, the wife of a county judge, who was floating in the waste of waters upon a small red barn. The dullest could infer from the approval he gave this act of his Uncle Henry, unwisely chivalrous as it might seem in view of the fact that whoever rescued the judge's wife farther down stream, would return her to the judge, while no one would return the hogs to Mr. Perkins—the dullest could infer from his praise that he was himself a chivalrous and tender young man whom any woman could trust.

The hour was become an hour and a half and both the pretty waitress and the eighth woman had grown very fidgetty. The waitress saw she was to beguile the tedious period of emprisonment by the tempest with no dalliance with Mr. Middleton. The eighth woman was worried by the absence of her escort. Mr. Middleton stepped to her side, where she stood staring out at the wind-swept street, and addressed her.

"Madame, it would almost seem as if some accident had detained your escort. May I not offer to call a cab and see you home? I have an umbrella with me."

The lady thanked him almost eagerly, saying that she would wait fifteen minutes more and at the elapse of that time, her escort not appearing, would gladly avail herself of his kind offer.

Twenty minutes later, they were whirling away northward. Crossing the Wells Street bridge, they turned eastward only a few blocks from the river. The rain had suddenly ceased. The wind having relaxed nothing of its fierceness, it occasionally parted the scudding clouds high over head to let glimpses of the moon escape from their wrack, and Mr. Middleton saw he was in a region whence the invasion of factories and warehouses had driven the major portion of the inhabitants forth, leaving their dwellings untenanted, white for rent signs staring out of the empty casements like so many ghosts. The lady signaling the driver to stop, Mr. Middleton assisted her to alight, and glanced about him. Here the work of exile had been very thorough. Not yet had the factories come into this immediate neighborhood, but the residents had retreated before the smoke of their advancing lines, leaving a wide unoccupied space behind the rear guard. Up and down the street, in no house could he perceive a light. The moon shining forth clear and resplendent, its face unobstructed by clouds for a moment, he saw stretching away house after house with white signs that grimly told their loneliness. Indeed, quite deserted did appear the very house to whose door they splashed through the pools in the depressions of the tall flight of stone steps. The lady threw open the door and stepped briskly in, and her footfalls rang sharply upon a bare floor and resounded in a hollow echo that told it was an empty house!

An empty house! An empty house! What danger might lurk here and how easy might losels lure victims to their door! Mr. Middleton paused on the threshold, staring into the gloom, but whatever irresolute thoughts he had entertained of retreat were dispelled by the sound of a wail from the lady, and the sight of her face, white in the moonlight, as she rushed out to him.

"Oh, oh," she moaned, gibbering a gush of words which, despite their incoherence of form, in their tone proclaimed fear, consternation, and despair.

Lighting a match, Mr. Middleton stepped into the house. Standing in the little circle of dull yellow light, he saw beneath his feet windrows of dust and layers of newspapers that had rested beneath a carpet but lately removed, and beyond, dusk emptiness, and silence. He advanced, looking for a chandelier, but though he found two, the incandescent globes had been removed from them. Throwing a mass of the papers from the floor into the grate and lighting them, a bright glare brought out every corner of the room. There was nothing but the four bare walls.

"They have taken everything, everything!" cried the poor lady.

"Who?" asked Mr. Middleton, after the manner of his profession.

"Who? Would that I knew!—Thieves."

Mr. Middleton then realized she had been the victim of a form of robbery far too common, where the scoundrels come with drays and carry off the whole household equipment, in the householder's absence. That which had been done in comparatively well-populated quarters was easy of accomplishment on this deserted street.

Penetrated with compassion, he moved toward the unfortunate woman, who with an abandonment he had not expected of one so stately and reserved, threw herself upon his breast, weeping as though her heart would break.

"They have taken everything. How can I get along now! My piano is gone and how can I give lessons without it! I will have to go back to Peoria!"

Soothingly Mr. Middleton patted the weeping woman on the back. With infinite tenderness, he kissed her tear-bedewed cheeks and gently he laid her head upon his shoulder, and then with both arms clasped about her, he imparted to her statuesque figure a sort of rocking motion, crooning with each oscillation, "There, there, there, there," until the paroxysm of her grief abated and passed from weeping into gradually subsiding sobs, and he began to tell her that he would be only too happy to give his legal services to convict the villains when caught—as they surely would be. The lady by degrees becoming more cheerful and giving him a description of the stolen property, he discussed ways and means of recovering it, and to prevent her from relapsing into her former depressed condition, occasionally imprinted a consolatory salute upon her cheek, from which he had previously wiped the wet tracks of the tears that had now some time ceased gushing, for there had been a salty taste to the first osculations, which while not actually disagreeable, had not been to his liking.

At length, the lady not only ceased even to sigh, but even to talk, and yet remained leaning upon him, which was whether because she was weary, exhausted by grief, or whether because her supporter was such a good looking young man, is not evident. Doubtless it was true that at first her misery and unhappiness made her need the sympathetic caresses of any one within reach and that with the return of her equilibrium she continued to make this an excuse for enjoying without any reproach of impropriety a recreation which ordinarily the conventions of society would compel her to eschew. As for the rising light in the legal profession, he began to find the weight she leant upon him oppressive, and his occupation, delightful at first, palling and growing monotonous. The monotony he somewhat relieved by frequently kissing her, now on one velvet cheek, now on the other, and again her lips; slowly, one two, three, in waltz measure; and rapidly, one, two three, four, in two-step measure, when all at once in the midst of a sustained half note there came to him the reflection that this was no time of night for him to be there in the dark in a deserted house kissing a woman with whose social standing, whose very name, he was unacquainted. He was about to ask a few leading questions, when there was the sound of wheels in the street; a carriage stopped before the door.

Quickly extricating himself from the lady's arms, Mr. Middleton stepped to the door, only to see the carriage drive away, the sound of voices singing a solemn chant in a strange and unknown tongue floating back to him.

Wondering what all this could mean, he turned to find the lady standing at his side, silently regarding him in a wrapt manner.

"The hour is late," said she, in a hollow, mournful voice, "and I ought to be seeking some shelter where I can lay my head, but where, oh, where?"

The lady made a tragic gesture as she asked this question, and there in that lonely street with this lorn woman at this late hour of the night in the eerie light of the cloud-obscured moon, with the wind, now howling and now sobbing and moaning, Mr. Middleton felt very solemn indeed. But he pulled himself together and suggested a low-priced and respectable hotel not far away, and toward this they were faring when they passed a house which, unlike most of the others of the vicinity, bore signs of habitation, and unlike any of the others, had a light showing in a window. In fact, there was a light in every window of the two upper stories and in the windows of the first floor and even in the basement. Pausing to wonder at this unusual illumination, Mr. Middleton felt his arm suddenly clutched, and a voice which he would never have believed came from the lady, if there had been any one else present, grated into his ear, "It's him."

Though startled by this enigmatical utterance, he followed when she ascended two steps of the stoop for a better view in the uncurtained window. There, with his face buried in his hands, seated on a roll of carpeting with a tack hammer and saucer of tacks at his side, sat the mulierose man!

"This house was empty at four this afternoon," said the lady. "Heavens, that's my piano in the corner! That's my center table! I believe that's my carpet! That's my watercolor painting I painted myself! He's robbed me!"

Her voice rose to a shriek, and at the sound a woman's head popped out of the window above and the mulierose man came running to the door. He was in his shirt sleeves but wore a hat.

"You've robbed me, you've robbed me!" cried the lady.

"I haven't," said the mulierose man with the utmost composure. "I can explain it all satisfactorily. Come in. My Aunt Eliza is here and tea is ready. Where were you when I went back to the restaurant? They said you had gone. Where were you?"

To Mr. Middleton's surprise, the lady immediately quieted at the words of the mulierose man and instead of berating him, coughed nervously and hung her head sheepishly.

"Where were you?" repeated the man.

"At my house."

"All this time? With this young man?" There was a tinge of hardness and jealousy in the man's voice and he looked unpleasantly at Mr. Middleton. "What did you stay in that empty house all this time for? What-were-you-doing-there?"

Mr. Middleton was at his wit's end to supply a hypothesis to answer why the mulierose man, from being a criminal and object of the lady's just wrath, should suddenly have become an inquisitor, sitting in judgment upon her conduct.

"I—I—was afraid to start right away. It was dark in there and I was afraid this young man might take liberties. Indeed, he did try to kiss me."

With a roar, the mulierose man launched himself at Mr. Middleton, who dexterously stepping aside, had the satisfaction of seeing his assailant slip and fall on the wet sidewalk. The lady thereat raised a cry of great volume, which was taken up by the woman looking out of the window above, and Mr. Middleton thinking he could derive neither pleasure nor profit from remaining longer in that locality, fled incontinently.

Upon his arrival home and preparing for bed, he found that he was wearing a stiff hat made in Kansas City, bearing on the sweat-band a silver plate inscribed "George W. Dobson." The mulierose man and he had exchanged hats at the restaurant. The mulierose man now had the love philter.

It was not until four days had elapsed that Mr. Middleton found an opportunity to visit the street where these inexplicable events took place. The house where he had comforted the eighth woman was still empty. At the house whence the mulierose man had issued, a very unprepossessing old woman, with a teapot in her right hand, was opening the front door to admit a large yellow cat whom she addressed as "Mahoney," an appellation which, while not infrequently the family name of persons of Irish birth or descent, is of very seldom application to members of the domestic cat tribe, Felis cattus.

Wondering greatly at the chain of unusual events, he went about his business. You may depend upon it that he gave much thought to an attempted solution of all these mysteries. But whether or no it was after all only a series of events commonplace in themselves, but seeming mysterious because of their fortuitous concatenation, or he really had trodden upon the hem of a web of strange and darksome, perhaps appalling, mysteries, he has never been able to say. He was minded to speak of these things to the emir and get his opinion on them.

Upon reflection, remembering how the philter had not been of any avail in the case of the young lady of Englewood, he thought, despite the explanation which might be offered for this failure, that the emir might be embarrassed at hearing of the failure of the charm, and accordingly he said nothing when once more he sat in the presence of the urbane and accomplished prince of the tribe of Al-Yam. Having handed him a bowl of delicately flavored sherbet, Achmed began to narrate The Unpleasant Adventure of the Faithless Woman.

THE UNPLEASANT ADVENTURE OF THE FAITHLESS WOMAN.

DR. AUGUST MOEHRLEIN, Ph. D., was a professor of the languages and religions of India. A man of great gravity of countenance and of impressive port, he was popularly reputed to have a complete knowledge of the occult learning of the adepts of India, that nebulous and mysterious philosophy which irreducible to the laws of nature as recognized by Occidentals, is by them pronounced either magic and feared as such, or ridiculed and despised as pretentious mummery and deluding prestidigitation. There was a legend among the students of his department that he was wont to project himself into the fourth dimension and thus traveling downtown, effect a substantial saving of street-car fare. This is clearly impossible, for the yogis do not thus move about in their own persons. It is only the astral self that flies leagues through the air with the rapidity of thought, only the spiritual essence, the living man's ghost flying abroad while the living man's corpse lies inanimate at home. But even this, Dr. August Moehrlein could not do, for the yogis do not initiate men of Western nations into their mysteries. Dr. Moehrlein's knowledge of the occult of India was wholly empirical. He knew that certain things were done and could recount them, but as to how they were done, he could tell nothing. It must not be thought that of all the marvelous and awe-compelling things the yogis of India are accustomed to do, none can be assigned to any other origin than cunning legerdemain and hypnotism, or to the exercise of supernatural powers. Many of them are due to a strange and wonderful knowledge of nature which the science of the Occident has not yet reached in all its boasted advance. Yet when once explained, the Westerner understands some of these phenomena and is able to repeat them. Into this region of the penumbra of science and exact knowledge the researches of Dr. Moehrlein had taken him a little way and it was this that had gained him his reputation among his pupils as a thaumaturgist.

Along with the learning which this country has imported from Germany have come some customs to which the savants of both that country and this ascribe a certain fostering influence, if not a creative impulse, highly advantageous to the national scholarship. It is the habit of the university men of Germany to foregather of nights in the genial pursuit of drinking beer, and many of the notable theories which German scholarship has propounded are to be directly attributed to this stimulating good fellowship known as kommers. Indeed, when one has imbibed twelve or fourteen steins of beer and sat in an atmosphere of tobacco smoke for some hours, his mind attains a clarity, a sense of proportion, a power of reflection, speculation, and intuition which enables him to evolve those notable theories for which German scholarship is so famous. It is under the intellectual stimulus of the kommers, when the foam lies thick in the steins and blue clouds of tobacco smoke roll overhead, that the great classical scholars of Germany perceive that the classical epics, the Iliad, the Odyssey, the Aeneid, are but the typifying of the rolling of the clouds in the empyrean, the warfare of the foam-crested waves dashing upon the land, that the metamorphoses and amours of the gods and all the myths of the elder world, are but the mutations of the clouds and the fanciful figures they take on and the metamorphoses and hurryings of the ever-changing sea with its foam forms and the shadows that lie across its unquiet surface. Wonderful indeed is the scientific imagination that thus accounts for, classifies, and labels the imagination of the poets, which otherwise we might think a thing defying classification, an inspiration, a creative genius taking nothing from a dim suggestion of the cold clouds and sea, but weaving its tales from the suggestion of human lives and human passions. Wonderful indeed is the good sense of the rest of the world in accepting unquestioned these important discoveries of German scholars in the beer kellars, which well might be called the laboratories of the classical department of the German universities.

Dr. August Moehrlein was a staunch advocate of the advantage of the kommers as an adjunct to every thoroughly organized university. If he could not gather others for a kommers, he would hold a kommers all by himself, or perchance with the barkeeper. Needless to say that the name of Moehrlein was attached to many valuable and plausible theories which America received as the last word on the subject treated; needless to tell you that the various gods of India had been identified with the sun, moon, and more important stars, and that it was conclusively shown that the Sanskrit romancers had written their tales by merely looking at the clouds and the sea. Would that this accomplishment of the ancients had not gone from us and that the moderns might write as the ancients by merely looking at the clouds and the sea. Dr. Moehrlein was an upholder of the kommers. But his wife, though German-born, behaved like a very Philistine and objected to his constant and unwavering attendance upon these occasions of intellectual uplift. For as the doctor added to the knowledge of the world, he added to his weight. He had identified Brahma with the sun, but had drunk his face purple in the intellectual effort. In his search for the suggestions of the tale of Nala, he had acquired a paunch very like a bag. Mrs. Moehrlein was accustomed to shrink from the approach of the victim of the pursuit of knowledge. As for him, he would have liked to caress and fondle her. To him there was always present a remembrance of her early beauty and the golden mist of memory shone before his eyes and he did not see that she was a heavy, middle-aged woman with coarse features and coarse figure. Animal beauty she had once had. The beauty had utterly flown, but the animal all remained. She had a shifty and wandering eye, burned out and lusterless, that told of dreams that were of men, men who these many years had not included her husband, grotesque figure that he was, ugly as a satyr in one of the myths suggested by the clouds and the sea.

It was a pleasant day of the last of May, in the mating season of birds, when the world was warm and throbbing with young life. The eminent Asiatic scholar looked across the lunch table, regarding his wife with wistful sadness as she refreshed herself with boiled cabbage.

"Do you know the day? It is thirty years since Hilsenhoff went into the box; thirty years since we have been man and—woman."

"Ah, yes, this is the anniversary. Thirty years, thirty years. Poor young Hilsenhoff."

She said these words with a tinge of sadness that was almost regret and this did not escape the doctor.

"One might fancy you were sorry. Yet it was your own doing. I was young and handsome then. A Hercules, young, full of life, late champion swordsman of the university, a rising light in the realm of learning, as well as a figure in society. You were the beautiful wife of tutor Hilsenhoff, the buxom girl with the form of a Venus and the passion of that goddess as well, tied to a thin, pallid bookworm ten years your senior, neglecting his pouting wife with blood full of fire for the pages of the literature of Hindoostan, prating of the loves of Ganesha and Vishnu, when a goddess awaited his own neglectful arms. So when on the day when he stepped into the box, leaving us the sole repository of the secret of his whereabouts—that the mutton-headed police might not interfere with the success of his experiment by preventing what they might think practically suicide—you said to let him stay."

"I was twenty and he thirty," mused the woman. "Poor young Hilsenhoff."

"Young! I was twenty-three—and a man."

"Dead or alive, he is young Hilsenhoff to me. He was thirty when last I saw him."

"Dead or alive? What are you thinking of?"

An idea had been taking shape in the woman's mind without her realizing it. It had grown from her own words, rather than had the words sprung from the idea.

"Why, if a man be brought into a condition where all bodily functions are suspended and he is as he were dead, and remain in this condition for months and be brought out of it no more harmed than if he had slept overnight, why may it not be years, instead of months? Has any man ever proved that, in this condition, one may not live on indefinitely?" she said.

"No man has ever proved that one cannot, but what is more important, no man has ever proved that one can. No man has ever proved beyond shadow of doubt that one may not fashion wings and fly, but no man has ever demonstrated that one can. In India, only one man has ever tried to continue in a state of suspended animation for over six months, and that was the rajah who, condemned to death by the English, ostensibly died before the soldiers could come to carry out the sentence and was brought out of his tomb and restored to life three days after a new British viceroy had proclaimed a general amnesty to all past offenders. The period was eight months. If the viceroys had not been changed for a number of years, we might have learned more concerning the length of the period in which a man may continue in the semblance of death without it becoming reality. No, these twenty-five years has Hilsenhoff been bones."

"Then let us take them out and bury them."

"No, no. Then would I feel like a murderer indeed. I left him in there for you. Now let his bones rest there for sake of me."

But the woman had become possessed of an idea which in turn possessed her, a dream, for which like all mankind, she would fight harder than for any substantiality, for no reality can be so glorious as a dream.

"But there was the man at Sutlej, the man who had himself buried in a wheat field for the edification of Alexander the Great, there to remain until a wheat crop had passed through its stages from sowing until harvest."

"The man at Sutlej!" exclaimed the doctor impatiently. "That a man was thus buried, the pages of Quintus Curtius's history show, and the Macedonian armies suddenly retreating from India, he was forgotten and not one, but two thousand wheat harvests have been garnered over his burial place."

"But the article in the Revue Des Deux Mondes, telling how he had been found," objected the woman faintly.

The doctor looked at her in amazement.

"What will not people do to believe that which they wish to believe. You, you, you!—do you ask me concerning that lie in the Revue Des Deux Mondes? Oh, woman, woman! When did your memory of the details of that hoax fail you? Not longer ago than ten minutes. A lying Frenchman said he was on his way to France with a resuscitated contemporary of Alexander the Great and that a full account of the matter would be published in two or three months. Hilsenhoff left the duration of his stay in the box at my discretion, enjoining me, however, that he should not be taken out before the Frenchman had published the full account of the Sutlej case, for we would then have many interesting comparisons in his behavior and response to the restorative methods used, and the reaction and response of this man buried two thousand years to the same methods for restoring suspended animation. The Frenchman never arrived with his man. It was all a lie. Yet by following Hilsenhoff's solemn injunctions to the letter, we had an excuse to leave him as dead, and you insisted that we should do so, and I, weak and infatuated with your ripe beauty, agreed. You said that we would leave him in his self-chosen sleep and that he should be our lodger. And so he has been and we have never called him to breakfast in all these thirty years. We have even brought him to America with us and he sleeps. Ah, no, we did not slay him. We but obeyed his commands."

"Poor young Hilsenhoff. And I am his wife and he is but thirty years old and I am fifty. Heigho!"

"Woman, you will drive me crazy," said the great annotator of the Upanishads, and he left for a kommers with the nearest barkeeper.

"As if you did not drive me crazy, you obese, misshapen wine skin! you bloated, blue-faced sot!" said the woman. "I deserted young Hilsenhoff for you, Hilsenhoff with his delicate cheeks and his soft yellow hair, and he is mine and I am his and I will let him out of the box and we will live together in love, the dear young thing. What if he does study sometimes? I shall not mind. He need not always sit with me in love's dalliance."

All at once it came home to her that if Moehrlein maintained the resuscitation of Hilsenhoff was impossible and charged her with believing it possible because she wished to believe it so, it might also be true that he did not believe it possible because he did not wish to so believe. The burned out eyes that told of dreams of men, men who these many years had not included her husband, smoldered with a sudden fire. With a song in her heart, she was up and bustling about. She filled a brazier with coals and got a frying-pan and wheat-cake batter, and a razor and a crocheting hook—ah, she knew how the process of restoring suspended animation was practised. She lumbered up into the third story with her burdens, into the room where slept the lodger. Not for fifteen years had anyone looked into that sleeping chamber. The blinds and curtains, all were drawn, the dust lay thick under foot. She let in the light of day at every window. There sat the box in the middle of the floor, hooped with bands of iron and with the great seal of the University of Bonn stamped upon the lock. She broke the seal and turned the lock and then sank down in a sudden faintness of heart. Indeed, how loath she was to put an end to the dream that had just now filled her whole being with rapture, and what else would it be but to put an end to it when she delved into that box? She would go away and let herself dream on a few days more before putting the matter to its final test, perhaps never doing so. Thus she reasoned, and yet her hand, as she sat before the box with averted face, rose as if impelled by the volition of another intelligence, over the edge of the box, down to the mass of wool and wadding, through it to the wrappings and swathings in the middle, through the wrapping, and felt—the thrill of unimaginable joy ran through her. It was not bones, it was not bones!

Into the room of the lodger came Dr. August Moehrlein. The coals of the brazier were out, the batter had been turned into cakes, the razor was covered with hair, four waxen plugs lay by the crocheting hook. The process was over. The sleeper was awake and there he stood, his delicate face yet pinched with sleep and his eyes heavy, but alive and young, young Hilsenhoff with his soft yellow hair and mild blue eyes. On the floor before him in an attitude of adoration, knelt the woman who in the view of the law, was his wife, her eyes burned out no longer, but aflash with youthful passion. But in her eyes alone was there youth. Nothing of youthful archness and coquetry was there in her gaze, only greed, the sickening fondness of an aging woman for a young man. In a daze, he stared at her and heard her clumsy compliments, her vulgar protestations of love, things which the ripe beauty of her youth might have condoned, but now were nauseating. He saw her heavy jowls and sensual lips, the thick nose and all the revenges of time upon a once beautiful body that had clothed an ugly soul. He looked at his own rusty clothing, stiff and hard and creased in a thousand wrinkles, and into the mildewed nest where the mould from the moisture of his own body grew thick and green and horrible. He gazed at Dr. Moehrlein, the one-time Adonis of Bonn, and he shuddered, and which of what he looked at, or whether all, made him do so, he could not tell.

Old men like young women, but so do old women hanker after young men. The life companion of Moehrlein embraced Hilsenhoff's knees. With smirkings and grimacings and leers that started his shudders afresh, she told him all. She confessed her crime and abased herself, but now they would begin life again, and she croaked forth a string of allurements from a throat that had known too many rich puddings. Oh, who shall describe her transports! Never before had every fiber of her being been so penetrated with joy! A young husband, oh, a young husband! By as much as Moehrlein had once surpassed him, did Hilsenhoff now surpass Moehrlein a hundred fold. And young, young, young! She was like to fall on her face in her ecstasy. The discarded and despised Moehrlein stood by and paid, if never before, the price of his villainy. There is a contempt of man for man and a contempt of woman for woman, but the contempt of woman for man——

One sleeps and is unconscious, but nonetheless by some subtle sense is aware of the passage of time, and the thirty years that he had slept, pressed upon young Hilsenhoff and his soul yearned to take up life again. He looked at the companions of his youth, that youth which was still his and had gone from them, and he looked at the place where he had lain for a third of a century, thick with damp green mould. Outside the song of birds was calling him, the rustle of green leaves and the glorious sunlight, the world renewing its life with the warm throbs of the year's youth, and putting from him forever his living grave and the woman and her paramour, he rushed into the joyous springtide.

Now why, my friend, descend into the hell of repinings and rage and heart-gnawings of that woman he left behind? Or why tell of the misery of the learned Dr. Moehrlein? She has no comfort whatsoever, but the doctor has the solace of his kommers, so let us wish that his beer may be forever flat, his wieners mildewy, and the mustard mouldy like the horrible nest of young Hilsenhoff.

WHAT BEFELL MR. MIDDLETON BECAUSE OF THE SEVENTH GIFT OF THE EMIR.

"I DID not know that such things were possible," said Mr. Middleton, when Prince Achmed had concluded the tale of the episode of the two Orientalists and the faithless woman. "Do I understand that the person in this condition is asleep?"

"It is not consistent with strict scientific accuracy to say the person is asleep," said the emir; "for the vital processes are entirely in abeyance and the subject is devoid of any evidence of life. The pulse is still, for the heart no longer beats and all the blood having retreated to that inmost citadel of the body, the skin has the pallor of death. Only in a little spot upon the crown is there any sign of life. Here is a place warm to the touch and the first and most important operation in restoring the suspended animation, is to send this vital warmth forth from where it still feebly simmers, coursing once more through the body's shrunken channels. This is accomplished by shaving the crown and applying thereto a succession of piping hot pancakes. The tongue has been curved back over the entrance to the throat. You reach into the mouth and with a finger pull the tongue back into place. Plugs of wax in the nostrils and ears are removed, and in a very short time the subject is as well as ever."

"It is very interesting," murmured Mr. Middleton.

"Since you find it so, let me present you with a little treatise upon the subject written by a Mohammedan hakim, or doctor of medicine, after studying several cases of the kind at Madras, which is in India," and at his bidding, Mesrour brought him a small portable writing desk from which he took a manuscript scroll inscribed in the Arabic language. "The first page," said Prince Achmed, "contains a few thoughts upon the superiority of the Moslem faith over all others and a discussion of the follies, inconsistencies, not to say evils of them all when compared with that perfect religious system declared to men by the Prophet of Mecca," and having in an orotund voice given Mr. Middleton some idea of the contents of this page by quoting a number of sentences, the prince handed him the sheet, which was inscribed upon one side only. The emir continuing to give a summary of what the hakim set forth in the remaining pages, and handing over each sheet as he finished it, Mr. Middleton wrote in short-hand upon the blank side of each preceding sheet what the emir culled from the one following, omitting, of course, the contents of the first sheet, both because he had nothing to write upon while the emir was quoting from that one, and because its theology was entirely contrary to all Mr. Middleton held, and, in his eyes, ridiculous and sacrilegious. When the emir had done, Mr. Middleton had in his possession a succinct account of the process of inducing a condition of suspended animation and of the means of restoring the subject to his normal state. It was his intention to write an article from his notes for some Sunday paper, and putting the hakim's treatise in his pocket, and thanking his host for the entertainment and instruction as well as the gift, he sought his lodgings.

Mr. Middleton had now been admitted to the bar for some time. But the firm of Brockelsby and Brockman did not therefore raise his salary. They made greater demands upon his endeavors than before, for he was now able to handle cases in court, but they did not raise his salary, nor did they employ him upon cases where he was able to distinguish himself, or learn new points of law and gain forensic ability. He was employed upon humdrum and commonplace cases that were a vexation to his spirit without any compensating advantage of pecuniary reward or experience. While he felt that his self-respect and on one hand his self-interests impelled him to resign his connection with Brockelsby and Brockman, on the other hand, the very course his employers pursued made such retirement temporarily inexpedient. For the trivial cases he handled could neither gain him reputation enough or make him friends enough to warrant him in setting up for himself, nor would they attract the attention of other firms and result in offers at an increased salary. He was in a measure forced to remain with Brockelsby and Brockman, hoping they would be moved to pay him according to his worth and dreaming of some contingency which might place in his hands the management of an important case with the resulting enhancing of his reputation.

On the morning after he had received the dissertation of the hakim, Mr. Middleton arose with the first streak of dawn, minded to seek the office and write his projected article before the time for his regular duties should arrive. As he opened the door of the main office, his ear was saluted by a low grunting sound, and there in evening dress was Mr. Augustus Alfonso Brockelsby, reclining in a big chair, asleep, if one could with propriety call the stupor in which he was sunk, sleep. The disorder of his garments, the character of his sternutations, the redness of his face, and above all, the odor he distilled upon the chill morning air, made patent to Mr. Middleton the disgusting fact that the senior member of the firm was drunk. On the table before the unconscious man was a note from Mr. Brockman informing him that he had been unexpectedly called to Lansing, Michigan, and would not be back for a week and that therefore he, Brockelsby, would have to attend to the important case of Ralston versus Hippenmeyer, all by himself. Mr. Middleton at once set about bringing his employer into a condition where he could attend to his affairs, for the case of Ralston versus Hippenmeyer was a very important one indeed, and as Mr. Middleton had briefed the case himself and had his sympathies greatly excited for Johannes Hippenmeyer, he was very anxious that their client should not lose for default of any effort he could make. But his heart was heavy as he brought towels and a basin of cold water from the wash-room, for after he had done his very best, Brockelsby would still be far from the proper form, his brain befogged, his speech thick, and the counsel for the other side would make short work of him.

Mr. Middleton had never tried to sober a drunken man, but he had an indistinct recollection of hearing that a towel wet with cold water, wrapped around the head was the best remedial agent. As he soaked the towels, he could not but compare the difference between this chill restorative and the hot cakes in the tale of the emir, and on a sudden there came to him a thought that sent all the gloom from his face. He dropped the towels, he dropped the basin, and he opened the treatise of the hakim and feverishly refreshed his memory of the details of an operation sometimes practised in India.

An hour and a half had passed when Mr. Middleton finished. Mr. Augustus Brockelsby still sat in the revolving chair, but he was no longer disturbing the air with his unseemly grunts. He was, in fact, absolutely silent, absolutely still. The keenest touch could feel no pulsation in his wrist, the keenest eye could detect no agitation of his chest, the keenest ear could hear no beating from the region of the heart. For a moment as he gazed upon the result of following the instructions set down by the hakim, Mr. Middleton felt a little clutch of fear. But he was reassured by the lifelike appearance of the learned jurisconsult and by the fact that the induction into his present state had been attended by none of the manifestations that accompany death.

"Now," said Mr. Middleton, addressing the unconscious form of Augustus Brockelsby, "now there will be no chance of you appearing in court in the case of Ralston versus Hippenmeyer. I will not restore you until it is all over. I will now have the long coveted opportunity to plead an important case and as I have studied it so carefully, I shall win. There will now be no chance that poor little Hippenmeyer will suffer from your disgraceful and bestial habits, for in spite of the best that could be done for you, you would be in no fit condition to plead a case this afternoon. And when I bring you to at fall of night, you will think you have been drunk all day. But where will I keep you in the meantime?"

This was a most perplexing problem. There were no closets in the suite of offices. There were no boxes, no desks big enough to conceal a man and Mr. Middleton's brow was beginning to contract as he struggled with the problem, when suddenly the stillness of the room was disturbed by some one smiting the door. Not a sound made he, for his heart had stopped beating as completely as Brockelsby's. What should he do, what should he do? The paralysis of fear answered for him and supplied the best present plan and he did nothing. Then came a voice, a voice calling him by name, the voice of Chauncy Stackelberg.

"Open up, old man, open up. I know you are there, for I heard you knocking around before I rapped and you dropped your handkerchief outside the door. Open up, or I'll shin right over the transom, for I must see you," and still preserving silence, Mr. Middleton heard a sound as of a man essaying to stand on the door knob and grasp the transom above. He rushed to the door, unlocked it, and opening it just enough to squeeze through, shut it behind him and thrust the key in the lock.

"Keep still, keep still. You'll wake the old man. I can't let you in."

"Was that him, slumped down in the chair? Must be tired to sleep in that position. Say, old chap, you were my best man, and now I want you again."

"Want me to draw up papers for a divorce?" said Mr. Middleton, gloomily. How was he going to get rid of this inopportune fellow?

"Shut up," said Chauncy Stackelberg. "It's a boy, and I want you to come up to the christening next Sunday and be godfather. You don't know how happy I am. Say, come on down and get a drink."

Ten minutes before, Mr. Middleton had been convinced that drink was a very great curse, but he accepted this invitation with alacrity, naming a saloon two blocks away as the one he considered best in that vicinity. He surmised that the happy father would hardly offer to come back with him from such a distance, and the surmise was correct. As he reascended to the office, with him in the elevator were two gentlemen, one of whom he recognized as Dr. Angus McAllyn, a celebrated surgeon who had two or three times come to the office to see Mr. Brockelsby and the other as Dr. Lucius Darst, a young eye and ear specialist who within the space of but a few days had established his office in the building. To neither of these gentlemen, however, was Mr. Middleton known.

"I want you to get off on this floor with me," said Dr. McAllyn to his medical confrere. "I may want your assistance a bit. You see," he went on, as they got out of the elevator and started down the corridor with Mr. Middleton just behind, "we had a banquet last night of the Society of Andrew Jackson's Wars, and my friend Brockelsby got too much aboard. He was turned over to me to take to his home, but just as we were leaving, I received an urgent call. So the best I could do was to drive by here and start him toward his office and go on. He could navigate after a fashion and doubtless spent the night all right in his office, and I would take no farther trouble with him but for the fact that he has an important case to-day. So I want to fix him up, and as I haven't much time, you can be of service to me."

"Ah, ha," said Mr. Middleton to himself, "I'll just lie low until they have given up trying to get in and have gone."

But they did not go away. To his consternation, they opened the door and walked in, for though he had put the key in the lock when he had closed the door behind him to parley with Chauncy Stackelberg, he had walked away without turning it! They would find Mr. Brockelsby! Great though Dr. McAllyn was, he would hardly be likely to recognize a condition of suspended animation. Unless Mr. Middleton confessed, there was danger that the famous forensic orator would be buried alive. And if he confessed, what would the consequences be to himself? The fact that in whatever event he would lose his place and be a marked and disgraced man, was the very least thing to consider. He was threatened with far more serious dangers than that. First, there would be the vengeance the law would take upon him for meddling with and tampering with medical matters. But even if he had been a physician, would the medical faculty look otherwise than with horror upon this rash and wanton experimenting with the strange and unholy practices of India? Even a medical man would be arrested for malpractice and for depriving a fellow being of the use of his faculties. The penitentiary stared him in the face.

He could not endure not to know what was taking place within. He must have knowledge of everything in order to know what moves to make and when to make them. He let himself through the outer door of Mr. Brockman's private office, and by taking a position by the door communicating between this office and the main office, he could hear everything in safety.

"Shall I send for an undertaker?" asked Dr. Darst.

At these chilling words, Mr. Middleton was about to open the private office door and rush in and confess all. He had begun to place the key in the lock, when a joyful thought stayed his hand. Let them bury Mr. Brockelsby. He would dig him up. He laughed noiselessly in his intense relief. But hark, what does he hear?

"Darst, this is an unusual case."

"Yes?" said Dr. Darst mildly.

"A strange, a remarkable case. Darst, if we do not examine this case, we are traitors to science. Darst, we must take him to the medical school.

When we are through, we'll sew him all again and bring him back here, or leave him almost any place where he can be found easily. He will be just as good to bury then as now, nobody hurt, and the cause of science advanced. Observe, Darst, dead, absolutely dead, yet with no rigor mortis. Dead, and yet as if he slept. If need be, we will pursue to the inmost recesses of his being the secret of his demise."

Mr. Middleton was nigh to falling to the floor. The succession of hope and fear had taken from him all resolution. Of what use would it be to exhume Mr. Brockelsby after the doctors had cut him up? The impulse to rush in and confess had spent itself and he was now cravenly drifting with the tide. All judgment, all power of reflection had departed from him. He was now only a pitiable wretch with scarcely strength to stand by the door and listen, unable to originate any thought, any action.

"How are you going to get him out of here?" asked Dr. Darst.

"In a box. You don't suppose I'd carry him down and put him in a hack?"

"But suppose they get to looking for him? It is known that he came here. A box goes out of here to be taken to the medical school, a long box that might hold a man. You and I are the ones who hire the men who carry the box."

"Who said a long box that might hold a man? It will be a short, rather tall box, packing-case shape. Remember, he is as limber as you are and can be accommodated to any position. He will be put in it sitting bolt upright. It will be only half the length of a man, with nothing in its shape to suggest that it might hold a man. Who said take it to the medical school from here? I hire a drayman to take a box to the Union Depot. He dumps it there on the sidewalk near the places for in-going and out-going baggage. Ostensibly going to carry it as excess baggage. We fiddle around until he goes, then call up some other drayman in the crowd hanging about and take a box just arrived from Milwaukee, St. Paul, any place the drayman wants to think, out to the college. As for the inquiry that will be made concerning the whereabouts of Brockelsby, rest easy on that point. He frequently goes off on sprees of several days' duration and his absence from home is of such common occurrence that his wife won't begin to hunt him up until we are through with him and have got him back here, or have dumped him in front of some building with his neck broken, showing that he fell out of some story above."

All this Mr. Middleton heard as he leaned against the door jamb, swallowing, swallowing, with never a thing in his mouth since the night before, yet swallowing. He heard Dr. Darst go after a box. He heard men deposit it in the corridor outside. He heard the two doctors take it in when the men had gone. He heard it go heavily out into the corridor again after a long interval. He heard more men come, come to carry it away, and he pulled himself together with a supreme effort and followed. He saw the box loaded on a dray. With his eye constantly on it, he threaded his way through the crowd on the sidewalk, followed it on its way across the river to the Union Depot. With never a hope in his heart that anything could possibly occur to save him from a final confession and its consequences, humanlike postponing the evil hour as long as he could.

The box was dumped upon the sidewalk before the depot. The two medical men stood leaning upon it, waiting for the drayman to depart. The evil moment had arrived. Once away from the depot, in the less congested streets in the direction of the medical college, the dray would go too fast for him to follow. He approached. He must speak now. No, no. He need not follow the dray. That was not necessary. He could get to the medical school before they could have time to do injury to Mr. Brockelsby. It would be safe to let the box get out of his sight for that little time. He would tell at the medical college.

"Yes, as soon as we get him there," said Dr. McAllyn, "we'll put him in the pickle."

Mr. Middleton sprang forward and put an appealing hand upon the shoulder of either doctor. With a sudden start that caused him to start in turn, each wheeled about. For a moment, he could say nothing and stood with palsied lips while they gave back his stare. Gave back his stare? All at once his mouth came open and these were the words he heard issue forth:

"Sirs, I arrest you for stealing the body of Mr. Augustus Alfonso Brockelsby, attorney-at-law."

He who had just now been an abject, grovelling wretch, was of a sudden come to be a lord among men. The practitioners making no reply, he continued:

"Are you going to be sensible enough to make no trouble, or shall I have to call yonder officer?"

Mr. Middleton considered this quite a master stroke. By the assumption of a pretended authority over the neighboring policeman he would forestall any possibility of resistance and question as to what authority he represented. But he need have had no fears on this score. The doctors were too alarmed to do otherwise than submit to his pleasure, too thoroughly convinced that none but a detective could have had knowledge of the contents of the box. But Dr. McAllyn did attach a significance to what Mr.

Middleton had said, a significance natural to one so well acquainted with the devious ways of the great city as he was.

"Well," he said, with a sardonic smile, "you needn't call in help. We stand pat. How much is it going to cost us?"

Then did Mr. Middleton perceive he was delivered from a dilemma, a dilemma unforeseen, but which even if foreseen, he could not have forearmed against. After he had arrested the doctors, how would he have disposed of them and the box containing Mr. Brockelsby? How could he have released the doctors and carried off the box in a manner that would not excite their suspicions? If he had, in pretended leniency and soft-heartedness told them they were free, the absence of any apparent motive for this action would have instantly caused them to suspect that for some unknown and probably unrighteous reason, he desired possession of the body of Mr. Brockelsby and thus would ensue a series of complications that would make the ruse of the arrest but a leap from the frying pan into the fire. But now Dr. McAllyn had supplied the motive.

"Sirs," said Mr. Middleton, with an air of virtue that was well suited to the character of the sentiments he now began to enunciate, "you deserve punishment. You have been taken in the act of committing a crime that is particularly revolting,—stealing a corpse. Dr. McAllyn, you have been apprehended in foul treason against friendship. You have stolen the body of a comrade. You have meditated cruel and shocking mutilation of this body, giving to the horror-stricken eyes of the frantic widow the mangled and defaced flesh that was once the goodly person of her husband, leaving her to waste her life in vain and terrible speculations as to where and how he encountered this awful death with its so dreadful wounds."

"It was for the sake of science," interpolated Dr. McAllyn, in no little indignation. "If from the insensible clay of the dead we may learn that which will save suffering and prolong existence for the living, well may we disregard the ancient and ridiculous sentiment regarding corpses, a relic of the ancient heathen days when it was believed that this selfsame body of this life was worn again in another world."

"I will not engage in an antiquarian discussion with you, sir, as to the origin of this sentiment. Suffice to say it exists and is one of the most powerful sentiments that rules mankind. You have attempted to violate it, to outrage it. However you may look upon your action, the penitentiary awaits you. Yet one can well hesitate to pronounce the word that condemns a fellow man to that living death. It is not the mere punishment itself. The dragging years will pass, but what will you be when they have passed? We no longer brand the persons of convicts, but none the less does the iron sear their souls and none the less does the world see with its mind's eye the scorched word 'convict' on their brows, so long as they live. In the capacity of judge, were I one, I might use such limit of discretion as the law allows in making your punishment lighter or heavier, but the disgrace of it, no one can mitigate. Therefore, that you may receive some measure of the punishment you deserve, and yet not be blasted for life, I will accept a monetary consideration and set you free."

"Oh, you will, will you?" said Dr. McAllyn. "How much lighter or heavier will you in your capacity as judge make this impost?"

"I will not take my time in replying to your slurs in kind. You, Dr. McAllyn, as the one primarily responsible, as the leader who induced Dr. Darst to enter this conspiracy, as the one most to be reproached, in that Mr. Brockelsby was your friend, as the one by far the most able to pay, you shall pay $1,200. Dr. Darst shall pay $200. This is a punishment by no means commensurate with your crime. By this forfeit, shall you escape prison and disgrace."

"Of course you know that I have no such sum as that about me," said Dr. McAllyn. "I will write you a check."

"I am not so green as I look," said Mr. Middleton, assuming an easy sitting posture upon the box containing the mortal envelope of Mr. Brockelsby. "You may dispatch Dr. Darst with a check to get the money for you and himself. You will remain here as a hostage until his return."

Accordingly, Dr. Darst departed and Mr. Middleton sat engrossed in reflection upon the chain of unpleasant circumstances that had forced upon him the unavoidable and distasteful rôle of a bribe-taker. Yet how else could he have carried off the part he had assumed? How else could he have obtained custody of Mr. Brockelsby? And surely the doctors richly deserved punishment. It was not meet that they should go scot free and in no other way could he bring it about that retribution should be visited upon them.

"It is all here," said Mr. Middleton, when he had counted the bills brought by Dr. Darst. "I shall now see that Mr. Brockelsby is taken back to the office whence you took him."

"Pardon me," said Dr. Darst, "how in the world did you know we took him from his office? How did you ferret it all out?"

"I cannot tell you that," said Mr. Middleton. "I shall take him back to the office. He will be found there later in the day, just as you found him. You are wise enough to make no inquiries concerning him, to watch for no news of developments. Indeed, to make in some measure an alibi, should it be needed, you had better leave town by next train for the rest of the day. If it were known you were with Mr. Brockelsby at any time, might it not be thought that you were responsible for the condition he was found in?"

The doctors boarded the very next train, and Mr. Middleton, serene in the knowledge that no one would disturb him now, had the box taken back and set up in the main office. A slight thump in the box as it was ended up against the wall, caused Mr. Middleton to believe that Mr. Brockelsby was now resting on his head, but he resolved to allow this unavoidable circumstance to occasion him no disquiet. Going to a large department store where a sale of portières was in progress, he purchased some portières and a number of other things. The portières he draped over the box, concealing its bare pine with shimmering cardinal velvet and turning it into the semblance of a cabinet. Lest any inquisitive hand tear it away, he placed six volumes of Chitty and a bust of Daniel Webster upon the top and tacked two photographs of Mr. Brockelsby upon the front. Confident that no one would disturb the receptacle containing his employer, he went into court and after a short but exceedingly spirited legal battle in which he displayed a forensic ability, a legal lore, and a polished eloquence which few of the older members of the Chicago bar could have equalled, he won a signal victory.

Although it was not his intention to set about restoring Mr. Brockelsby until an hour that would ensure him against likelihood of interruption, he returned to the office to see if by any untoward mischance anybody could have interfered with the box. To his surprise, he found Mrs. Brockelsby seated before that object of vertu with her eye straying abstractedly over the cardinal portières, the photographs of Mr. Brockelsby, the bust of Daniel Webster, and the volumes of Chitty.

"Oh, Mr. Middleton," exclaimed the lady. "Mr. Brockelsby did not come home to-day and they tell me he wasn't in court."

"No, he was not in court," said Mr. Middleton.

"Oh, where, oh, where can he be!" moaned Mrs. Brockelsby.

Mr. Middleton being of the opinion that this question was merely exclamatory, ejaculatory in its nature, of the kind orators employ to garnish and embellish their discourse and which all books of rhetoric state do not expect or require an answer, accordingly made no answer. He was, nevertheless, somewhat disturbed by the poor lady's grief and wished that it were possible to restore her husband to her instantly.

"Oh, I have wanted to see him so, I have wanted him so! Oh, where can he be, Mr. Middleton! I must find him. I cannot endure it longer. I will offer a reward to anyone who will bring him home within twenty-four hours, to anyone who will find him. Oh, oh, oh, oh! I will give $200. I will give it to you, yourself, if you will find him. Write a notice to that effect and take it to the newspaper offices."

This great distress on the part of the lady was all contrary to what Dr. McAllyn had said concerning her indifference to the absence of her spouse and caused Mr. Middleton to feel very much like a guilty wretch. As he wrote out the notices for the papers, he reiterated assurances that Mr. Brockelsby would turn up before morning, while the partner of the missing barrister continued her heartbroken wailing and the cause of it all was driven well-nigh wild.

"Oh, if you only knew!" she said, as Mr. Middleton was about to depart for the newspaper offices. "Day after to-morrow, I am going to Washington to attend a meeting of the Federation of Woman's Clubs. That odious Mrs. LeBaron is going to spring a diamond necklace worth two thousand dollars more than mine. Augustus must come home in time to sign a check so I can put three thousand dollars more into mine."

A great load soared from Mr. Middleton's mind and blithe joy reigned there instead.

"Mrs. Brockelsby, I'll leave no stone unturned. I'll bring you your husband before breakfast," and escorting the lady to her carriage and handing her in with the greatest deference and most courtly gallantry, he set forth for one of the more famous of the large restaurants which are household words among the elite of Chicago. Mr. Middleton had never passed its portals, but with fourteen hundred dollars in his pocket and two hundred more in sight, he felt he could afford to give himself a good meal and break the fast he had kept since the evening before, for in the crowded events of the day, he had found time to refresh himself with nothing more substantial than an apple and a bag of peanuts, or fruit of the Arachis hypogea.

As he sat down at a table in the glittering salle-à-manger, what was his great surprise and even greater delight, to see seated opposite, just slowly finishing his dessert—a small bowl of sherbet—habited in a perfectly-fitting frock coat with a red carnation in the lapel, the urbane and accomplished prince of the tribe of Al-Yam. Having exchanged mutual expressions of pleasure at this unexpected encounter, Mr. Middleton, overjoyed and elated at the successes of the day, began to pour into the ears of the prince a relation of the events that had resulted from the gift of the treatise of the learned hakim of Madras, which is in India. He told everything from the beginning to the end.

"In the morning," he said in conclusion, "I take Mr. Brockelsby home in a cab and get the two hundred dollars."

"Alas, alas!" said Achmed mournfully, his great liquid brown eyes resting sorrowfully upon Mr. Middleton. "What a corrupting effect the haste to get rich has upon American youth. My friend, it cannot be that you intend to take the two hundred dollars?"

"But I find old Brock, don't I?'

"That is precisely what you do not do. You know where he is. You put him there. How can you say you found him?"

"All right, I won't do it," said Mr. Middleton, abashed at Achmed's reproof, a reproof his conscience told him was eminently deserved.

"I thank Allah," said the prince, "that I am an Arab and not an American. The fortunes of my line, its glories, were not won in the vulgar pursuits of trade, in the chicanery of business, in the shady paths of speculation, in the questionable manipulation of stocks and bonds. It was not thus that the ancient houses of the nobility of Europe and the Orient built up their honorable fortunes. Never did the men of my house parley with their consciences, never did they strike a truce with their knightly instincts in order to gain gold. Ah, no, no," mused the prince, looking pensively up at the gaily decorated ceiling as he reflected upon the glories of his line; "it was in the noble profession of arms, the illustrious practice of warfare that we won our honorable possessions. At the sacking of Medina, the third prince of our house gained a goodly treasure of gold and precious stones, and founded our fortune. In warfare with the Wahabees, we acquired countless herds and the territories for them to roam upon. By descents across the Red Sea into the realms of the Abyssinians, we took hundreds of slaves. From the Dey of Aden we acquired one hundred thousand sequins as the price of peace. In the sacking of the cities of Hedjaz and Yemen and even the dominions of Oman, did we gallantly gain in the perilous and honorable pursuit of war further store of treasure. Ah, those were brave days, those days of old, those knightly days of old! Faugh, I am out of tune with this vile commercial country and this vile commercial age."

The prince arose as he uttered these last words and in his rhapsody forgetting the presence of Mr. Middleton, without a farewell he stalked through the great apartment, absentmindedly, though gracefully twirling a pair of pearl gray gloves in the long sensitive fingers of his left hand. A little hush fell upon the brilliant assemblage and many a bright eye dwelt admiringly upon the elegant person, so elegantly attired, of the urbane and accomplished prince of the tribe of Al-Yam.

For some time Mr. Middleton sat plunged in abstraction, toying with the three kinds of dessert he had ordered, as he meditated upon the words of the emir. At last rousing himself, he had finished the marrons glacées and was about to begin upon a Nesselrode pudding, when he heard himself addressed, and looking up saw before him a young woman of an exceedingly prepossessing appearance. She was richly dressed with a quiet elegance that bespoke her a person of good taste. Laughing, roguish eyes illuminated a piquant face in which were to be seen good sense, ingenuousness and kindness, mingled with self-reliance and determination. Mr. Middleton knew not whether to admire her most for the beautiful proportions of her figure, the loveliness of her face, or the fine mental qualities of which her countenance gave evidence. With a delightful frankness in which there was no hint of real or pretended embarrassment, she said:

"Pray pardon this intrusion on the part of a total stranger. I have particular reasons for desiring to know the name and station of the gentleman who left you a short time ago, and knowing no one else to ask, have resolved to throw myself upon your good nature. I will ask of you not to require the reasons of me, assuring you that they are perhaps not entirely unconnected with the welfare of this gentleman. I observed from your manner toward one another that you were acquaintances and that it was no chance conversation between strangers. He is, I take it, an Italian."

Without pausing to reflect that the emir might not be at all pleased to have this young woman know of his identity, Mr. Middleton exclaimed hastily and with a gesture of expostulation:

"Oh, no! He is not a Dago," and then after a pause he remarked impressively, "He is an Arab," and then after a still longer pause, he said still more impressively, "He is the Emir Achmed Ben Daoud, hereditary prince of the tribe of Al-Yam, which ranges on the borders of that fertile and smiling region of Arabia known as Yemen, or Arabia the Happy."

"He is not a Dago!" said the young woman, clasping her hands with delighted fervor.

"He is not a Dago!" said another voice, and Mr. Middleton became aware that at his back stood a second young woman scarcely less charming than the first. "He is not a Dago!" she repeated, scarcely less delighted than the first.

Mr. Middleton arose and assumed an attitude which was at once indicative of proper deference toward his fair questioners and enabled him the better to feast his entranced eyes upon them. Moreover, on all sides he observed that people were looking at them and he needed no one to tell him that his conversation with these two daughters of the aristocracy was causing the assemblage to regard him as an individual of social importance.

He gave the emir's address upon Clark Street and after dwelling some time upon his graces of person and mind, related how it was that this Eastern potentate was resident in the city of Chicago in a comparatively humble capacity.

"His brother is shut up in a vermillion tower."

"Vermillion, did you say?" breathlessly asked the first young lady.

"Oh, how romantic!" exclaimed the second young lady. "A tower of vermillion! Is he good looking, like this one? Do you suppose he will come here? Oh, Mildred, I must meet him. And the imam of Oman is going to give the vermillion tower to the brother, when he is released. We could send one of papa's whalebacks after it. What a lovely house on Prairie Avenue it would make. 'The Towers,' we would call it. No, 'Vermillion Towers.' How lovely it would sound on a card, 'Wednesdays, Vermillion Towers.' We must get him out. Can't we do it?"

"If it were in this country," said Mr. Middleton, "I would engage to get him out. I would secure a writ of habeas corpus, or devise other means to speedily release him. But unfortunately, I am not admitted to practice in the dominions of Oman. But I do not pity the young man. One could well be willing to suffer incarceration in a tower of vermillion, if he knew he were an object of solicitude to one so fair as yourself. One could wear the gyves and shackles of the most terrible tyranny almost in happiness, if he knew that such lovely eyes grew moist over his fate and such beauteous lips trembled when they told the tale of his imprisonment."

Now such gallant speeches were all very well in the days of knee-breeches and periwigs, but in this age and in Chicago, they are an anachronism and the two young ladies started as if they had suddenly observed that Mr. Middleton had on a low-cut vest, or his trousers were two years behind the times, and somewhat curtly and coolly making their adieus, they sailed rapidly away, leaving Mr. Middleton—who was not the most obtuse mortal in the world—to savagely fill with large pieces of banana pie the orifice whence had lately issued the words which had cut short his colloquy with the two beauties. He deeply regretted that in his association with Prince Achmed he had fallen into a flowery and Oriental manner of speech and resolved henceforth to eschew such fashion of discourse.

The clocks were solemnly tolling the hour of midnight when Mr. Augustus Alfonso Brockelsby rubbed his eyes and sat up in the revolving chair in the main office of his suite. Mr. Middleton was standing near, hastily putting away a razor. A warm odor lay on the still air of the room.

"Hello, isn't it daylight yet?" asked Mr. Brockelsby. The hot cakes that had but lately been applied to his shaven crown, seemed to have dispelled the fogs of intoxication and he was master of himself.

"It is twelve o'clock," said Mr. Middleton.

"Twelve! Why, it was three when I left the banquet table. Twelve!"

"Twelve," said Mr. Middleton, pointing gravely to the clock on the desk.

"It—is—twelve. Don't tell me it is the day after."

"I am compelled to do so. You were at the banquet of the Sons of Andrew Jackson's Wars, twenty-four hours ago."

"Great Scott!" exclaimed Mr. Brockelsby, thrusting his hands through his hair, or rather making the motion of doing so. "Great Scott!" he repeated, "I am bald-headed. What the devil have I been into? Where the devil have I been?"

"I found you here this morning. Your wife has been here."

"Oh, lord! Oh, lord! What did she say when she saw me dead to the world—and bald-headed?"

"She did not see you. I had concealed you."

"Good boy, good boy."

"She offered me two hundred dollars reward to bring you home," and Mr. Middleton related all that Mrs. Brockelsby had said.

"It would be all off when she saw me bald-headed. What the devil wouldn't she suspect? I don't know. I would say I didn't know where I had been. That would certainly sound fishy. It would sound like a preposterous excuse to cover up something pretty questionable. People don't go out in good society and get their heads shaved. She's pretty independent and uppish now. She said the next time she knew of me cutting up any didoes, she would get a divorce. She comes into two hundred thousand from her grandfather's estate in six months and she's pretty independent. Say, my boy, can't you take a check for the money she wants? She's going to Washington to-morrow. Tell her I went out of town and sent the money. I will go out of town. But the boys will see my bald head. Where do you suppose I was? What sort of crowd was I with? I must have a wig. You must get it for me. The boys would josh me to death, and if the story got to my wife it would be all off. I'll go to Battle Creek and get a new lot of hair started."

Mr. Middleton sat down and wrote busily for a moment. He handed a sheet of paper to Mr. Brockelsby.

"What's this? You resign? You're not going to help me out?"

"I am no longer in your employ. I will undertake to do all you ask of me for a proper compensation, say one hundred and fifty a day for two days."

"What?" screamed Mr. Brockelsby. "This is robbery, extortion, blackmail."

"It is what you often charge yourself. Very well. Get your own wig and be seen on the streets going after it. Leave your wife to wonder why I do not come to report what progress is made in the search for you and to start a rigorous investigation herself. I am under no obligations not to ease her worry, to calm her disturbed mind by telling her I have found you. She'll be hot foot after you then."

"She'd spot the wig at once. It would fool others, but not her. She'd see I had been jagged. You've got me foul. I'll have to accede to your terms. You'll not give me away?"

"Sir, I would not, in this, my first employment as an independent attorney, be so derelict to professional honor, as to betray the secrets of my client. We have chosen to call this three hundred dollars—a check for which you will give me in advance—payment for the services I am about to perform. In reality, I consider it only part of what you owe for the miserably underpaid services of the past three years."

As Mr. Middleton wended his way homeward, it was with some melancholy that he recalled how, on previous occasions when good fortune had added to his stock of wealth, he had rejoiced in it because he saw his dreams of marriage with the young lady of Englewood approaching realization more and more. But now they had drifted apart. Not once had he seen her since that fatal night. On several evenings he had made the journey to Englewood and walked up and down before her house, but not so much as her shadow on the curtain had he seen. Let her make the first move toward a reconciliation. If she expected him to do so after her treatment of him, she was sadly mistaken.

THE ADVENTURE OF ACHMED BEN DAOUD.

BEING curious to hear of the young ladies who had inquired concerning the emir in the restaurant, and to learn what their connection with that prince might be, Mr. Middleton repaired to the bazaar on Clark Street on the succeeding night. But the emir was not in. Mesrour apparently having experienced one of those curious mental lesions not unknown in the annals of medicine, where a linguist loses all memory of one or more of the languages he speaks, while retaining full command of the others—Mesrour having experienced such a lesion, which had, at least temporarily, deprived him of his command of the English language, Mr. Middleton was unable to learn anything that he desired to know, until bethinking himself of the fact that alcohol loosens the thought centers and that by its agency Mesrour's atrophied brain cells might be stimulated, revivified, and the coma dispelled, he made certain signs intelligible to all races of men in every part of the world and took the blackamore into a neighboring saloon, where, after regaling him with several beers, he learned that only an hour before an elegant turnout containing two young women, beautiful as houris, had called for the emir and taken him away.

"He done tole me that if I tole anybody whar he was gwine, he'd bowstring me and feed mah flesh to the dawgs."

Mr. Middleton shuddered as he heard this threat, so characteristically Oriental.

"Where was he going?" he inquired with an air of profound indifference and irrelevance, signalling for another bottle of beer.

The blackamore silently drank the beer, a gin fizz, and two Scotch highballs, his countenance the while bearing evidence that he was struggling with a recalcitrant memory.

"'Deed, I doan' know, suh," said Mesrour finally. "He never done tole me."

Though Mr. Middleton called three times during the next week, he did not find the emir in. Nor could Mesrour give any information concerning his master's whereabouts. However, in the society news of the Sunday papers, appeared at the head of several lists of persons attendant upon functions, one A. B. D. Alyam, and this individual was included among those at a small dinner given by Misses Mildred and Gladys Decatur. As Mildred was the name of one of the young ladies who had accosted him in the restaurant, Mr. Middleton felt quite certain that this A. B. D. Alyam was none other than Achmed Ben Daoud, emir of the tribe of Al-Yam.

On the tenth day, Mesrour informed Mr. Middleton that the emir had left word to make an appointment with him for seven o'clock on the following evening, at which time Mr. Middleton came, to find the accomplished prince sitting at a small desk made in Grand Rapids, Michigan, engaged in the composition of a note which he was inscribing upon delicate blue stationery with a gold mounted fountain pen. Arising somewhat abruptly and offering his hand at an elevation in continuity of the extension of his shoulder, the emir begged the indulgence of a few moments and resumed his writing. He was arrayed in a black frock coat and gray trousers and encircling his brow was a moist red line that told of a silk hat but lately doffed. "Give the gentleman a cup of tea," said he to Mesrour, looking up from the note, which now completed, he was perusing with an air that indicated satisfaction with its chirography, orthography, and literary style. At last, placing it in an envelope and affixing thereto a seal, he turned and ordering Mesrour to give Mr. Middleton another cup of tea, he lighted a cigarette and began as follows:

"This is the last time you will see me here. My lease expires to-morrow and my experience as a retail merchant, in fact, as any sort of merchant, is over. On this, the last evening that we shall meet in the old familiar way, the story I have to relate to your indulgent ears is of some adventures of my own, adventures which have had their final culmination in a manner most delightful to me, and in which consummation you have been an agent. Indeed, but for your friendship I should not now be the happy man I am. Without further consuming time by a preamble which the progress of the tale will render unnecessary, I will proceed.

"Last summer, I spent a portion of the heated term at Green Lake, Wisconsin. I know that sentiment in this city is somewhat unequally divided upon the question of the comparative charms of Green Lake and Lake Geneva and that the former resort has not acquired a vogue equal to that of the latter, but I must say I greatly prefer Green Lake. I have never been at Lake Geneva, it is true, but nevertheless, I prefer Green Lake.

"The hotel where I stayed was very well filled and the manager was enjoying a highly prosperous season. Yet though there were so many people there I made no acquaintances in the first week of my sojourn. Nor in the second week did I come to know more than three or four, and they but slightly. I was, in truth, treated somewhat as an object of suspicion, the cause of which I could not at first imagine. I was newer to this country and its customs and costumes there a year ago. Previous to starting for the lake, I had purchased of a firm of clothiers farther up this street, Poppenheimer and Pappenheimer, a full outfit for all occasions and sports incident upon a vacation at a fashionable resort. I had not then learned that one can seldom make a more fatal mistake than to allow a clothier or tailor to choose for you. It is true that these gentry have in stock what persons of refinement demand, but they also have fabrics and garments bizarre in color and cut, in which they revel and carry for apparently no other reason than the delectation of their own perverted taste, since they seldom or never sell them. But at times they light upon some one whose ignorance or easy-going disposition makes him a prey, and they send him forth an example of what they call a well-dressed man. More execrably dressed men than Poppenheimer and Pappenheimer and most of the other parties in the clothing business, are seldom to be found in other walks of life. In my ignorance of American customs, I entrusted myself to their hands with the result that my garments were exaggerated in pattern and style and altogether unsuited to my dark complexion and slim figure. But in the wearing of these garments I aggravated the original sartorial offence into a sartorial crime. With my golf trousers and white ducks I wore a derby hat. For nearly a week I wore with a shirt waist a pair of very broad blue silk suspenders embroidered in red. All at once I awoke to a realization that the others did not wear their clothes as I did and set myself to imitate them with the result that my clothes were at least worn correctly. The mischief was largely done, however, before this reform, and nothing I could do would alter the cut and fabric.

"My clothes were not the only drawbacks to my making acquaintances. I was entirely debarred from a participation in the sports of the place. I knew nothing of golf. A son of the desert, I could no more swim than fly, and so far from being able to sail a boat, I cannot even manage a pair of oars. I could only watch the others indulge in their divertissements, a lonely and wistful outsider.

"Yet despite all this, I could perceive that I was not without interest to the young ladies. Partially as an object of amusement at first, but not entirely that, even at first, for the sympathetic eyes of some of them betrayed a gentle compassion.

"Among the twenty or so young ladies at our hotel, were two who would attract the attention and excite the admiration of any assemblage, two sisters from Chicago, beautiful as houris. In face and figure I have never seen their equal. Their cheeks were like the roses of Shiraz, their teeth like the pearls of Ormuz, their eyes like the eyes of gazelles of Hedjaz. Before beholding these damosels, I had never realized what love was, but at last I knew, I fell violently in love with them both. Never in my wildest moments had I thought to fall in love with a daughter of the Franks. Nor had I contemplated an extended stay in this land, and before my departure from Arabia I had begun to negotiate for the formation of a harem to be in readiness against my return.

"But I soon began to entertain all these thoughts and to dally with the idea of changing my religion, abhorrent as that idea was. At first I had been comforted by the thought that I was in love with both girls in orthodox Moslem style. But reflecting that I could never have both, that they would never come to me, that I must go to them, becoming renegade to my creed, I tried to decide which I loved best. I came to a decision without any extended thinking. I was in love with Miss Mildred, the elder of the two sisters Decatur, daughters of one of Chicago's wealthy men, and this question settled, there remained the stupendous difficulty of winning her. For I did not even possess the right to lift my hat to these young ladies. My affair certainly appeared quite hopeless.

"In the last week of August, an Italian and his wife encamped upon the south shore of the lake with a small menagerie, if a camel, a bear, and two monkeys can be dignified by so large a title. He was accustomed to make the rounds of the hotels and cottages on alternate days, one day mounted on the dromedary and strumming an Oriental lute, on the others playing a Basque bagpipe while his bear danced, or proceeding with hand-organ and monkeys. He had been a soldier in the Italian colony of Massowah on the Red Sea, where he had acquired the dromedary—which was the most gigantic one I have ever seen—and a smattering of Arabic. English he had none, his wife serving as his interpreter in that tongue.

"The sight of the camel was balm to my eyes. Not only was it agreeable to me to see one of that race of animals so characteristic of my native land, but here at last was a form of recreation opened to me. I hired the camel on the days when the Italian was not using him and went flying about all over the country. Little did I suspect that I thereby became associated with the Italian in the minds of the public and that presently they began to believe that I, too, was an Italian and the real owner of the menagerie, employing Baldissano to manage it for me while I lived at my ease at the hotel. I was heard conversing with the Italian, and of course nobody suspected that I was talking to him in Arabic. It was a tongue unknown to them all and they chose to consider it Italian. Moreover, one Ashton Hanks, a member of the Chicago board of trade, at the hotel for the season, had said to the menagerie, jerking his thumb interrogatively at me, as I was busied in the background with the camel, 'Italiano? Italiano?' To which Baldissano replied, 'Si, signor,' meaning 'yes,' thinking of course that Hanks meant him. 'Boss? Padrone?' said Hanks again, and again the answer was, 'Si, signor.'

"So here I was, made out to be an Italian and the owner of a miserable little menagerie which I employed a minion to direct, while myself posing as a man of substance and elegant leisure. Here I was, already proven a person of atrocious taste in dress, clearly proclaimed of no social standing, of unknown and suspicious antecedents, a vulgarian pretender and interloper. But of course I didn't know this at the time.

"I was riding past the front of the hotel on the camel one day at a little before the noon hour, when I beheld her whom I loved overcome by keen distress and as she was talking rather loudly, I could not but be privy to what she said.

"'Oh, dear,' she exclaimed, clasping her hands in great worriment, 'what shall I do, what shall I do! Here I am, invited to go on a sail and fish-fry on Mr. Gannett's yacht, and I have no white yachting shoes to wear with my white yachting dress. I've just got to wear that dress, for I brought only two yachting dresses and the blue one is at the laundry. I thought I put a pair of white shoes in my trunk, but I didn't; I haven't time to send to Ripon for a pair. I won't wear black shoes with that dress. But how will I get white ones?'

"'Through my agency,' said I from where I sat on the back of the camel.

"'Oh,' said she, with a little start at my unexpected intrusion, her face lighting with a sudden hope, nevertheless. 'Were you going to Ripon and will you be back before one-thirty? Are you perfectly willing to do this errand for me?'

"'I am going to Ripon,' I said, 'and nothing will please me more than to execute any commission you may entrust to me. This good steed will carry me the six miles and back before it is time to sail. They seldom sail on the time set, I have observed.'

"She brought me a patent-leather dancing shoe to indicate the desired size, and away I went, secured the shoes, and turned homeward. While skirting a large hill that arises athwart the sky to the westward of the city of Ripon, I was startled by a weird, portentous, moaning cry from my mount. Ah, its import was only too well known to me. Full many a time had I heard it in the desert. It was the cry by which the camels give warning of the coming of a storm. While yet the eye and ear of man can detect no signs whatever of the impending outburst of nature's forces and the earth is bathed in the smiles of the sky, the camels, by some subtle, unerring instinct, prognosticate the storm.

"I looked over the whole firmament. Not a cloud in sight. A soft zephyr and a mellow sun glowing genially through a slight autumnal haze. Not a sign of a storm, but the camel had spoken. I dismounted at once. I undid the package of shoes. From my pocket I took a small square bit of stone of the cubical contents of a small pea. It was cut from the side of the cave where Mohammed rested during the Hegira, or flight of Mohammed, with which date we begin our calendar. This bit of stone was reputed to be an efficacious amulet against dangers of storms, and also a charm against suddenly falling in love. I placed it in the toe of the right shoe. Unbeknownst to her, Mildred would be protected against these dangers. I could not hope to dissuade her from the voyage by telling her of the camel's forewarning. Ashton Hanks was to be one of the yachting party and he had shown evidences of a tender regard for her. Retying the package, it was not long before I had placed it in the hands of Mildred. With a most winsome smile she thanked me and ran in to don the new purchases.

"The boat set sail and I watched it glide westward over the sparkling waves, toward the lower end of the lake, watching for an hour until it had slipped behind some point and was lost to sight. Then I scanned the heavens to see if the storm I knew must come would break before it was time for the yachting party to return. Low on the northern horizon clouds were mustering, their heads barely discernible above the rim of the world. But for the camel's warning I would not have seen them. The storm was surely coming. By six o'clock, or thereabouts, it would burst. The party was to have its fish-fry at six, at some point on the south shore. On the south shore would be the wreck, if wreck there was to be.

"With no definite plan, no definite purpose, save to be near my love in the threatening peril, I set out for the south shore. By water, it is from a mile and a half to three miles across Green Lake. By land, it is many times farther. From road to road of those parallel with the major axis of the lake, it is four miles at the narrowest, and it is three miles from the end of the lake before you reach the first north and south road connecting the parallels. Ten miles, then, after you leave the end of the lake on the side where the hotels are, before you are at the end on the other side. And then thirteen miles of shore.

"So what with the distance and the time I had spent watching the shallop that contained my love pass from my field of vision the afternoon had far waned when I had reached the opposite shore, and when I had descended to the beach at a point where I had thought I might command the most extensive view and discover the yacht, if it had begun to make its way homeward, the light of day had given place to twilight. But not the twilight of imminent night, the twilight of the coming tempest. For the brewing of a fearful storm had now some time been apparent. A hush lay on the land. A candle flame would have shot straight upward. Nature waited, silently cowering.

"To the northward advanced, in serried columns of black, the beetling clouds that were turning the day into night, the distant booming of aërial artillery thundering forth the preluding cannonade of the charge. Higher and higher into the firmament shot the front of the advancing ranks in twisting curls of inky smoke, yet all the while the mass dropped nearer and nearer to the earth and the light of day departed, save where low down in the west a band of pale gold lay against the horizon, color and nothing more, as unglowing as a yellow streak in a painted sunset. Against this weird, cold light, I saw a naked mast, and then a sail went creaking up and I heard voices. They had been shortening sail. By some unspent impulse of the vanished wind, or the impact of the waves still rolling heavily and glassily from a recent blow, the yacht was still progressing and came moving past me fifty or sixty feet from shore.

"I heard the voices of women expressing terror, begging the men to do something. Danger that comes in the dark is far more fearsome than danger which comes in the light. I heard the men explaining the impossibility of getting ashore. For two miles on this coast, a line of low, but unscalable cliffs rose sheer from the water's edge, overhanging it, in fact, for the waves had eaten several feet into the base of the cliffs. To get out and stand in front of these cliffs was to court death. The waves of the coming storm would either beat a man to death against the rocks, or drown him, for the water was four feet deep at the edge of the cliffs and the waves would wash over his head. For two miles, I have said, there was a line of cliffs on this coast, for two miles save just where I stood, the only break, a narrow rift which, coinciding with a section line, was the end of a road coming down to the water. They could not see this rift in the dusk, perhaps were ignorant of its existence and so not looking for it.

"The voices I had heard were all unfamiliar and it was not until the yacht had drifted past me that I was apprised it was indeed the craft I sought by hearing the voice of Mildred saying, with an assumed jocularity that could not hide the note of fear:

"'What will I do? All the other girls have a man to save them. I am the extra girl.'

"I drove my long-legged steed into the water after the boat none too soon, for the whistling of a premonitory gust filled the air. Quickly through the water strode the camel, and, with his lariat in my hand, I plumped down upon the stern overhang just as the mainsail went slatting back and forth across the boat and everybody was ducking his head. In the confusion, nobody observed my arrival.

"'She's coming about,' cried the voice of the skipper, Gannett. 'A few of these gusts would get us far enough across to be out of danger from the main storm.'

"But she did not come about. I could feel the camel tugging at the lariat as the swerving of the boat jerked him along, but presently the strain ceased, for the boat lay wallowing as before. Again a fitful gust, again the slatting of the sail, the skipper put his helm down hard, the boat put her nose into the wind, hung there, and fell back.

"'She won't mind her helm!'

"'She won't come about!'

"'She acts as if she were towing something, were tied to something!'

"'What's that big rock behind there? Who the devil is this? And how the devil did he get here?'

"In the midst of these excited and alarmed exclamations came the solemn, portentous voice of the camel tolling out in the unnatural night the tocsin of the approaching hurricane.

"'It's the Dago!' cried Gannett, examining me by the fleeting flash of a match. 'It's his damned camel towing behind that won't let us come about. Pitch him overboard!'

"'Oh, save me!' appealed Mildred.

"There she had been, sitting just in front of me and I hadn't known it was she. It was not strange that she had faith that I who had arrived could also depart.

"'Selim,' I called, pulling the camel to the boat. I had never had a name for him before, but it was high time he had one, so now I named him. 'Selim,' and there the faithful beast was and with Mildred in my arms, I scrambled on to his back and urged him toward the rift in the wall of cliff.

"As if I had spurned it with my foot, the boat sprang away behind us, a sudden rushing blast filling her sails and laying her almost over, and then she was out of our sight, into the teeth of the tempest, yelling, screaming, howling with a hundred voices as it darted from the sky and laid flat the waves and then hurled them up in a mass of stinging spray.

"In fond anticipation, I had dwelt upon the homeward ride with Mildred. A-camelback, I was, as it were, upon my native heath, master of myself, assured, and at ease. I had planned to tell her of my love, plead my cause with Oriental fervor and imagery, but before we reached shore the tempest was so loud that she could not have heard me unless I had shouted, and I had no mind to bawl my love. Worse still, when once we were going across the wind and later into it, I could not open my mouth at all. We reached the hotel and on its lee side I lifted her down to the topmost of the piazza steps. I determined not be delayed longer. If ever there was to be a propitious occasion, it was now when I had rescued her from encompassing peril. I retained hold of her hand. She gave me a glance in which was at least gratitude, and I dared hope, something more, and I was about to make my declaration, when she made a little step, her right foot almost sunk under her and she gave an agonized cry and hobbling, limping, hopping on one foot, passed from me across the piazza to the stairs leading to the second story, whither she ascended upon her hands and knees.

"That wretched stone from the cavern where Mahommed slept in the Hegira! How many times during the day had she wanted to take her shoe off? She would ascertain the cause of her torment, she would lay it to me. It had indeed been an amulet against sudden love. I was the man whose love it had forefended.

"'Gannett's yacht went down and all aboard of her were drowned,' said one of the bellboys to me. 'Everybody in the hotel is feeling dreadful.'

"'How do you know they are drowned?'

"'Everybody in the hotel says so. I don't know how they found out.'

"'What's that at the pier?' said I.

"The lights at the end of the pier shone against a white expanse of sail and there was a yacht slowly making a landing.

"Someone came and stood for a moment in an open window above me and there floated out the voice of one of the sisters Decatur, but which one, I could not tell. Their voices were much alike and I had not heard either of them speak very often.

"'Do you think that one ought to marry a person who rescues her from death, when he happens to be a Dago and cheap circus man into the bargain? I certainly do not.'

"Which one was it? Which one was it? Imagine my feelings, torn with doubt, perplexity, and sorrow. Was it Mildred, replying scornfully to some opinion of her sister, or was it the sister taking Mildred to task for saying she wished or ought to marry me? How was I to know? Could I run the risk of asking the girls themselves?

The emir paused, and it was plain to be seen from the workings of his countenance that once more he was living over this unhappy episode.

"I can well imagine your feelings and sympathize with them," said Mr. Middleton. "There you sat in the encircling darkness, asking yourself with no hope of an answer, 'Was it Mildred? Was it her sister? Was it Mildred contemptuously repudiating the idea of marriage with me, or the sister haughtily scoffing at some sentiments just professed by Mildred? But I should not have spent too long a time asking how I was to know. I should put the matter to the test and had it out with Mildred, Miss Mildred, I should say."

The emir looked steadily at Mr. Middleton. There was surprise, annoyance, perhaps even vexation in his gaze. With incisive tones, he said:

"How could you so mistake me? Ours is a line whose lineage goes back twelve hundred years, a noble and unsullied line. Could I, sir, think of making my wife, making a princess of my race, a woman who could entertain the thought of stooping to marry a Dago cheap circus man? Suppose I had gone to Mildred and had asked her if she had expressed herself of such a demeaning declaration? Suppose she had said, 'Yes,' then there I would have been, compromised, caught in an entanglement from which as a man of honor, I could not withdraw. The only thing to do was to keep silence. The risk was too great, I resolved to leave on the morrow. For the first time did I learn that I was believed to be a Dago and the proprietor of the little menagerie. This strengthened my resolve to leave.

"I left. Your happy encounter with the young ladies in the restaurant changed all. They learned from you that I was their social equal. They looked me up and apologized for their apparent lack of appreciation of my services and explained that they thought me a Dago circus man. I learned that neither of them believed in a mesalliance, that the question I had heard was a rhetorical question merely, one not expecting an answer, much used by orators to express a strong negation of the sentiments apparently contained in the question. But I have not yet learned which girl it was who asked the question. It is entirely immaterial and I don't think I shall try to find out, even after I am married, for of course you have surmised I am to be married, to be married to Mildred."

"Yes, another American heiress marries a foreign nobleman," said Mr. Middleton, with a bitterness that did not escape the emir.

"Permit me to correct a popular fallacy," said the emir. "Nothing could be more erroneous than the prevalent idea that American girls marry foreign noblemen because attracted by the glitter of rank, holding their own plain republican citizens in despite. Sir, it takes a title to make a foreigner equal to American men in the eyes of American women. A British knight may compete with the American mister, but when you cross the channel, nothing less than a count will do in a Frenchman, a baron in the line of a German, while, for a Russian to receive any consideration, he must be a prince.

"And now," said the emir, "my little establishment here being about to be broken up, I am going to ask you to accept certain of my effects which for sundry reasons I cannot take with me to my new abode. My jewels, hangings, and costumes, my wife will like, of course. But as she is opposed to smoking, there are six narghilehs and four chibouques which I will never use again. As I am about to unite with the Presbyterian church this coming Sunday, it might cause my wife some disquietude and fear of backsliding, were I to retain possession of my eight copies of the Koran. She may be wise there," said the emir with a sigh. "If perchance you should embrace the true faith and thereby make compensation for the loss of a member occasioned by my withdrawal———"

"That would not even matters up," interrupted Mr. Middleton, "for I am not a Presbyterian, but a Methodist."

"Oh," said the emir. "Well, there are five small whips of rhinoceros hide and two gags. My wife will not wish me to keep those, nor a crystal casket containing twenty-seven varieties of poisons. Then there are other things that you might have use for and I have not. I have sent for a cab and Mesrour will stow the things in it."

At that moment the cab was heard without and Mesrour began to load it with the gifts of the emir. At length he ceased his carrying and stood looking expectantly. With an air of embarrassment, and clearing his throat hesitatingly, the emir addressed Mr. Middleton.

"There is one last thing I am going to ask you to take. I cannot call it a gift. I can look upon your acceptance of it in no other light than a very great service. Some time ago, when marriage in this country was something too remote to be even dreamed of, I sent home for an odalisque."

The emir paused and looked obliquely at Mr. Middleton, as if to observe the effect of this announcement. That excellent young man had not the faintest idea what an odalisque might be, but he had ever made it a point when strange and unknown terms came up, to wait for subsequent conversation to enlighten him directly or by inference as to their meaning. In this way he saved the trouble of asking questions and, avoiding the reputation of being inquisitive and curious, gained that of being well informed upon and conversant with a wide range of subjects. So he looked understandingly at the emir and remarking approvingly, "good eye," the emir continued, much encouraged.

"To a lonely man such as I then was, the thought of having an odalisque about, was very comforting. Lonely as I then was, an odalisque would have afforded a great deal of company."

"That's right," said Mr. Middleton. "Why, even cats are company. The summer I was eighteen, everybody in our family went out to my grandfather's in Massachusetts, and I stayed home and took care of the house. I tell you, I'd been pretty lonely if it hadn't been for our two cats."

"But now I am going to be married and my wife would not think of tolerating an odalisque about the house. She simply would not have it. The odalisque arrived last night, and I am in a great quandary. I could not think of turning the poor creature out perhaps to starve."

"That's right," said Mr. Middleton. "Some persons desiring to dispose of a cat, will carry it off somewhere and drop it, thinking that more humane than drowning it. But I say, always drown a cat, if you wish to get rid of it."

"Now I have thought that you, being without a wife to object, might take this burden off my hands. I will hand you a sum sufficient for maintenance during a considerable period and doubtless you can, as time goes on, find someone else who wants an odalisque, or discover some other way of disposal, in case you tire——"

"Send her along," said Mr. Middleton, cordially and heartily. "If worst comes to worst, there's an old fellow I know who sells parrots and cockatoos and marmosets, and perhaps he'd like an odalisque."

"I will send her," said the emir.

"So it's a she," quoth Mr. Middleton to himself. He had used the feminine in the broad way that it is applied indefinitely to ships, railways trains, political parties etc., etc., with no thought of fitting a fact.

"I will give you fifteen hundred dollars for her maintenance. Having brought her so far, I feel a responsibility——"

"But that is such a large sum. I really wouldn't need so much——"

"That is none too large," rejoined the emir. "I wish her to be treated well and I believe you will do it. At first, she will not understand anything you say to her, of course, but she will soon learn what you mean. The tone, as much as the words, enlightens, and I think you will have very little trouble in managing her."

"Is there a cage?" hazarded Mr. Middleton, "or won't I need one?"

"Lock her in a room, if you are afraid she will run away, though such a fear is groundless. Or if you wish to punish her, the rhinoceros whips would do better than a cage. A cage is so large and I could never see any advantage in it. But you will probably never have occasion to use even a whip. You will have but this one odalisque. Had you two or three, they might get to quarreling among themselves and you might have use for a whip. But toward you, she will be all gentleness, all submission."

Mr. Middleton and the emir then turned to the counting and accounting of the fifteen hundred dollars, and so occupied, the lawyer missed seeing Mesrour pass with the odalisque and did not know she had been put in the hack until the emir had so apprised him.

"She is in a big coffee sack," said the emir. "The meshes of the fabric are sufficiently open to afford her ample facility for breathing, and yet she can't get out. Then, too, it will simplify matters when you get to your lodgings. You will not have to lead her and urge her, frightened and bewildered by so much moving about, but pack her upon your back in the bag and carry her to your room with little trouble.

"And now," continued the emir, grasping Mr. Middleton's hands warmly, "for the last time do I give you God-speed from this door. I will not disguise my belief that our intimacy has in a measure come to an end. As a married man, I shall not be so free as I have been. I am no longer in need of seeking out knowledge of strange adventures. The tyrannical imam of Oman, who imprisoned my brother, is dead, and his successor, commiserating the poor youth's sorrows, has not only liberated him, but given him the vermillion edifice of his incarceration. This my brother intends to transmute into gold, for he has hit upon the happy expedient of grinding it up into a face powder, a rouge, beautiful in tint and harmless in composition, for the rock was quarried in one of the most salubrious locations upon the upper waters of the great river Euphrates. I trust I shall sometimes see you at our place, where I am sure I shall be joined in welcoming you by Mrs.—Mrs.—well, to tell the truth," said the emir in some slight confusion, "I don't know what her name will be, for it is obviously out of the question to call her Mrs. Achmed Ben Daoud, and she objects to the tribal designation of Alyam, which I had temporarily adopted for convenience's sake, as ineuphonious."

"Sir, friend and benefactor, guiding lamp of my life, instructor of my youth and moral exemplar," said Mr. Middleton, in the emotion of the moment allowing his speech an Oriental warmth which the cold self-consciousness of the Puritan would have forbade, had he been addressing a fellow American, "I cannot tell you the advantages that have flowed from my acquaintance with you. It was indeed the turning point of my life. The pleasure I will leave untouched upon, as I must alike on the present occasion, the profits.

Let me briefly state that they foot up to $3760. A full accounting of how they accrued, would consume the rest of the night, and so it must be good-bye."

As Mr. Middleton looked back for the last time upon that hospitable doorway, he saw the gigantic figure of Mesrour silhouetted against the dim glow beyond and there solemnly boomed on the night air, the Arabic salutation, "Salaam aleikoom."

WHAT BEFELL MR. MIDDLETON BECAUSE OF THE EIGHTH AND LAST GIFT OF THE EMIR.

GETTING into the hack and settling into the sole remaining vacant space Mesrour had left in loading the vehicle with the emir's gifts, Mr. Middleton was so preoccupied by a gloomy dejection as he reflected that a most agreeable, not to say inspiring and educating, intimacy was at last ended, that he reached his lodgings and had begun to unload his new possessions, before he thought of the odalisque. There lay the coffee sack lengthwise on the front seat and partially reclining against the side of the carriage. He was greatly surprised at the size of the unknown creature and began to surmise that it was an anthropoid ape, though before his speculations had ranged from parrots through dogs to domesticated leopards. Leaving the coffee sack until the last, he gingerly seized the slack of the top of the bag and proceeded to pull it upon his shoulders, taking care to avoid holding the creature where it could kick or struggle effectually, for despite all the emir had told him of the gentleness of the odalisque, he was resolved to take no chances. Whatever the creature was, she had slid down, forming a limp lump at the end of the bag, when he charily deposited it on the floor and turned to consult his dictionary before untying it. He was going to know what the creature was before he dealt with her further, a creature so large as that.

Odalisque. A slave or concubine in a Mohammedan harem!!

A woman!!!

Mr. Middleton tore at the string by which the bag was tied, full of the keenest self-reproach. The uncomfortable position during the long ride, the worse position in which she now lay. The knots refused to budge and snatching a knife, with a mighty slashing, he ripped the bag all away and disclosed the slender form of a woman crouched, huddled, collapsed, face downward, head upon her knees. Turning her over and supporting her against his breast in a sitting posture, Mr. Middleton looked upon the most loveliness, unhappiness, and helplessness he had ever beheld.

For a moment his heart almost stopped as he looked into the still face, but he saw the bosom faintly flutter, slow tears oozed out from under the long lashes of the closed lids, and the cupid's bow mouth gave little twitches of misery and hopelessness. With what exquisite emotions was he filled as he looked down upon the head pillowed upon his breast, with what sentiments of anger, with what noble chivalry!

A Moslem woman. A Moslem woman, who even in the best estate of her sex as free and a wife, goes to her grave like a dog, with no hope of a life beyond, unless her husband amid the joys of Paradise should turn his thoughts back to earth and wish for her there among his houris. But this poor sweet flower had not even this faint expectation, for she was no wife nor could be, slave of a Mohammedan harem. No rights in this world nor the next. Not even the attenuated rights which law and custom gave the free woman. No sustaining dream of a divine recompense for the unmerited unhappiness of this existence. A slave, a harem slave, wanted only when she smiled, was gay, and beautiful; who must weep alone and in silence, in silence, with never a sympathetic shoulder to weep upon after they sold her from her mother's side. Tied in a bag, going she knew not whither, thrown in a carriage like so much carrion, in these indignities she only wept in silence, for her lord, the man, must not be discomposed. Like the timorous, helpless wild things of the woods whose joys and sorrows must ever be voiceless lest the bloody tyrants of their domain come, who even in the crunch of death hold silence in their weak struggles, this poor young thing bore her sufferings mutely, for her lord, the man, must not be discomposed, choking her very breath lest a sob escape. Mr. Middleton, in a certain illuminating instinct which belongs to women but only occasionally comes to some men, saw all this in a flash without any pondering and turning over and reflecting and comparing, and he said to himself under his breath, not eloquently, but well, as there came home to him the heinousness of that abhorrent social system dependent upon the religious system of the Prophet of Mecca, "Damn the emir and Mohammed and the whole damned Mohammedan business, kit and boodle!"

In this imprecation there was a piece of grave injustice which Mr. Middleton would not have allowed himself in calmer mood, for the emir was about to become a member of one of the largest and most fashionable Presbyterian congregations in the city and ought not to have been included in an anathema of Moslemry and condemned for anything he upheld while in the benighted condition of Mohammedanism.

Mr. Middleton continuing to gaze, as who could not, upon that beautiful unhappy face, suddenly he imprinted upon the quivering lips a kiss in which was the tender sympathy of a mother, the heartening encouragement of a friend, and the ardent passion of a lover. The odalisque opened her lovely hazel eyes and seeing corroboration of all the touch of the kiss had told her, as she looked into eyes that brimmed with tears like hers, upon lips that quivered like hers, she let loose the flood gates of her woes in a torrent of sobs and tears, and throwing herself upon his shoulders, poured out her long pent sorrows in a good cry.

It was only a summer shower and the sun soon shone. She did not weep long. Too filled with wonder and surpassing delight was this daughter of the Orient in her first experience with the chivalry of the Occident. She must needs look again at this man whose eyes had welled full in compassion for her. She would court again his light and soothing caresses, his gentle ministrations, so different from the brutal pawing of the male animals of her own race, the moiety with souls. Ah, how poignantly sweet, how amazing, that which to her American sisters was the usual, the commonplace, the everyday!

She raised her head. Her tears no longer flowed, but her lips still quivered, in a pleading little smile; and her bosom still fluttered, in a shy and doubting joy, and in her mind floated a half-formed prayer that the genii whose craft had woven this rapturous dream, would not too soon dispel it.

Mr. Middleton gazed at her. He had never seen a face like that, so perfectly oval; never such vermillion as showed under the dusk of her cheeks and stained the lips, narrow, but full. What wondrous eyes were those, so large and lustrous, illumining features whose basal lines of classic regularity were softly tempered into a fluent contour. A circlet of gold coins bound her brow, shining in bright relief against the luxuriant masses of chestnut hair. A delicate and slender figure had she, yet well cushioned with flesh and no bones stood out in her bare neck.

Moved not by his own discomfort on the hard floor, but by the possible discomfort of the odalisque, Mr. Middleton at length raised her and conducted her to a red plush sofa obtained by the landlady for soap wrappers and a sum of money, which having turned green in places and therefore become no longer suitable for a station in the parlor, had been placed in this room a few days before. Upon this imposing article of furniture the two sat down, and though at first Mr. Middleton did no more than place his arm gently and reassuringly about the girl's waist and hold her hand lightly, in the natural evolution, progression, and sequence of events, following the rules of contiguity and approach—rhetorical rules, but not so here—before long the cheek of the fair Arab lay against that of the son of Wisconsin and her arm was about his neck and every little while she uttered a little sigh of complete, of unalloyed content. What had been yesterday, what might be to-morrow, she was now happy. As for Mr. Middleton, what a stream of delicious thoughts, delicious for the most part because of their unselfishness and warm generosity, flowed through his head. What a joy it would be to make happy the path of this girl who had been so unhappy, to lay devotion at the feet of her who had never dreamed there was such a thing in the world, to bind himself the slave of her who had been a slave.

Then, too, he luxuriated in the simple, elementary joy of possession and the less elementary joy of possession of new things, whether new hats, new clothes, new books, new horses, new houses, or new girls, and which is the cause why so many of us have new girls and new beaux. And when he looked ahead and saw only one logical termination of the episode, he swelled with a pride that was honest and unselfish, as he thought how all would look and admire as he passed with this lovely woman, his wife.

He could have sat thus the whole night through, but the girl must be tired, worn by the sufferings of this day and many before. He motioned toward the bed and indicated by pantomime that she should go to it. She would have descended to her knees and with her damask lips brushed the dust from his shoes, if she had thought he wished it, but she knew not what he meant by his gesturing and sat bewildered in eager and anxious willingness. So arranging the bed for her occupancy, he took her in his arms and bore her to it and dropped her in. The riotous blushes chased each other across her cheeks as she lay there with eyes closed, so sweet, so helpless, so alone.

For a little season he stood there gazing, gloating, enravished, like to hug himself in the keen titillation of his ecstasy and this was not all because this lovely being was his, but because he was hers.

Glancing about the room preliminarily to leaving, and wondering what further was to be done for the girl's comfort and peace of mind, he bethought him of an ancient tale he had once read. In this narration, fate having made it unavoidable that a noble lord should pass the night in a castle tower with a fair dame of high degree and there being but one bed in the apartment, he had placed a naked sword in the middle of the bed between them and so they passed the night, guarded and menaced by the falchion, for the nonce become the symbol of bright honor and cold virtue. Mr. Middleton had often wondered why the knight did not sleep on the floor, or outside the door, as he himself now intended doing. But it occurred to him that some such symbol might reassure the Arab damosel and having no sword, he drew one of the large pistols the emir had given him and approached the bed to lay it there.

The girl's eyes had now opened and Mr. Middleton started as he beheld her face. Once more the hunted, helpless look it had worn when first he had looked on it. But more. Such an utter fear and sickening unto death. But not fear, terror for herself. Fear for the death of an ideal, a fear caused by her misinterpretation of his intent with the pistol. It had not been real, it had not been real. He was as other men, the men of her world and all the world was alike and life not worth living. With a finesse he had not suspected he possessed, he laid the pistol on a pile of legal papers on a table at the bed's head, a pile whose sheets a suddenly entering breeze was whirling about the room. How obvious it was he had brought the pistol for a paper weight. Once more the girl was smiling as he drew the clothes over her, all dressed as she was, and kissing shut her drowsy eyes, he left her in her virginal couch.

On the mat before the door in the hallway without, he disposed himself as comfortably as he could. With due regard for the romantic proprieties, he tried to keep within the bounds of the mat. But it was too short, his curled up position too uncomfortable, and so he overflowed it and could scarcely be said to be sleeping on the mat. It was too late to arouse the landlady and although he was there by choice, it could not have been otherwise.

After snatches of broken sleep, after dreams waking and dreams sleeping, which were all alike and of one thing and indistinguishable, he was at length fully awake at a little before six and aware of an odor of tobacco smoke. Applying his nose to the crack of the door, he finally became convinced that it came from his room. Wondering what it could possibly mean, and accordingly opening the door, opening it so slowly and gradually that the odalisque could have ample time to seek the cover of the bed clothes, he stepped in.

There sat the odalisque on the edge of the bed, fully dressed, puffing away at his big meerschaum, blowing clouds that filled the room. On the table lay an empty cigarette box that had been full the night before. This had not belonged to Mr. Middleton, who was not a cigarette smoker and despised the practice, but had been forgotten by Chauncy Stackelberg on a recent visit. The fingers of her right hand were stained yellow, not by the cigarettes of that one box, but the unnumbered cigarettes of years. Mr. Middleton had not noticed these fingers the night before, but had been absorbed by her face, and this as beautiful, as piquant, as bewitching as before, looked up at him, the lips puckered, waiting, longing.

He stood there, stock-still, stern, troubled, dismayed.

She moved over, where she sat on the edge of the bed, with mute invitation, and Mr. Middleton continuing to stand and stare, she moved again and yet again, until she was against the headboard. And still he did not sit beside her, thinking all the time of the young lady of Englewood whose pure Puritan lips never had been and never could be defiled by cigarettes and tobacco. The young lady of Englewood, the young lady of Englewood, what a jewel of women was she and what a fool he had been and how unkind and inconsiderate! Recalled by a little snuffle from the odalisque, he saw the puckered lips were relaxing sorrowfully and fearing the girl would cry, he hastily sat down beside her and put his right arm about her. But he did not take the shapely hand that now laid down the meerschaum, and though her head fell on his shoulder and her breath came and went with his, he did not kiss her, for that breath was laden with tobacco. Nor did his fingers stray through those masses of silken hair, for he was sure they were full of the fumes of tobacco. There with his arm about the soft, uncorsetted form of that glorious beauty, her own white forearm smooth and cool about his neck, he was thinking of the young lady of Englewood.

Poor odalisque! Why cannot he speak to you and tell you? You would wash away those yellow stains with your own blood, if you thought he wished it. Forego tobacco? Why, you would cease to inhale the breath of life itself, for his sake.

Out of the grave came all the dead Puritan ancestors of Mr. Middleton, a long procession back to Massachusetts Bay. The elders of Salem who had ordained that a man should not smoke within five miles of a house, the lawgivers who had prescribed the small number, brief length, and sad color of ribbons a woman might wear and who forbade a man to kiss his wife on Sunday, all these righteous and uncomfortable folk stirred in Mr. Middleton's blood and obsessed him.

Fatima, Nouronhor, or whatever your name might be, my fair Moslem, why did fate throw you in with a Puritan? Yet I wot that had it been one from a strain of later importation from Europe, you had not been so safe there last night. The Puritans may be disagreeable, but they are safe, safe.

Part of this Mr. Middleton was saying over and over to himself—the latter part. The Puritans are safe. The young lady of Englewood was safe. She was good, she was beautiful, too, in her calm, sweet, Puritan way. He must see her at once, he would go—— A sigh, not altogether of content, absolute and complete, recalled to him the woman pressed against his side. She must be taken care of, disposed of. Asylum? No. Factory? No, no. Theater, museum? No, no, no. He would find some man to marry her. There must be someone, lots of men, in fact, who would marry a girl so lovely, who needn't find out she smoked until after marriage, or who would not care anyway. All this might take time. He would be as expeditious as possible, however. He called Mrs. Leschinger, the landlady, and entrusting the girl to her care, departed to visit a matrimonial agency he knew of.

He looked over the list of eligibles. He read their misspelled, crabbedly written letters. There was not one in the lot to whom a man of conscience could entrust the Moslem flower, even if she did smoke.

"There is apparently not one man of education or refinement in the whole lot," exclaimed Mr. Middleton.

"That's about right," said the president of the agency. "Between you and I, there ain't many people of refinement who would go at marrying in that way. You don't know what a lot of jays and rubes I have to deal with. Often I threaten to retire. But occasionally a real gentleman or lady does register in our agency. Object, fun or matrimony. Now I have one client that is all right, all right except in one particular. He is a man of thirty-five or six, fine looking, has a nice house and five thousand dollars a year clear and sure. But he's stone deaf. He wants a young and handsome girl. Now I could get him fifty dozen homely young women, or pretty ones that weren't chickens any longer, real pretty and refined, but you see a real handsome young girl sort of figures her chances of marrying are good, that she may catch a man who can hear worth as much as this Crayburn, which ain't a whole lot, or that if she does marry a poor young chap, he'll have as much as Crayburn does when he is as old as Crayburn. Now I'm so sure you'll only have your trouble for your pains, that I won't charge you anything for his address and a letter of introduction. I don't believe you have got a girl who will suit, for if you have, she won't take Crayburn. Here's his picture."

Mr. Middleton looked upon the photograph of a man who seemed to be possessed of some of the best qualities of manhood. It was true that there was a slight suspicion of weakness in the face, but above all it was kindly and sympathetic.

"A good looking man," said Mr. Middleton.

"Smart man, too," said the matrimonial agent. "He graduated from the university in Evanston and was a lawyer and a good one, until a friend fired off one of those big duck guns in his ear for a joke."

Taking the odalisque with him in a cab, Mr. Middleton was off for the residence of Mr. Crayburn.

"Will she have me?" asked Mr. Crayburn, when he had read Mr. Middleton's hastily penciled account of the main facts of his connection with the fair Moslem, wherein for brevity's sake he had omitted any mention of the fifteen hundred dollars the emir had given him for assuming charge of her.

"Of course," wrote Mr. Middleton.

"I never saw a more beautiful woman," exclaimed Mr. Crayburn. "By the way, have you noticed any predilections, habits, wants, it would be well for me to know about?"

"She smokes," wrote Mr. Middleton, not knowing why he wrote it, and wishing like the devil that he hadn't the moment he had.

"All Oriental women smoke. I will ask her not to as soon as she learns English."

Mr. Middleton was amazed to think that such a simple solution had not occurred to him. But he was glad it was so, for he had not been unscathed by Cupid's darts there last night and he might not now be about to visit the young lady of Englewood.

"Your fee," said Mr. Crayburn.

Mr. Middleton had not thought of this. He looked about at the handsomely furnished room. He thought of the five thousand dollars a year and the very much smaller income he could offer the young lady of Englewood. He thought of these things and other things. He thought of the young lady of Englewood; of the odalisque, toward whom he occupied the position of what is known in law as next friend. She sat behind him, out of his sight, but he saw her, saw her as he saw her for the first time, when, ripping the bag away, she lay there in her piteous, appealing helplessness.

"There is no fee. The maiden even has a dowry of fifteen hundred dollars. Please invest it in her name. Oh, sir, treat her kindly."

"Treat her kindly!" exclaimed the deaf man with emotion. "He would be a hound who could ill treat one so helpless and friendless, a stranger in a strange land, whose very beauty would be her undoing, were she without a protector."

Much relieved, Mr. Middleton prepared to depart and the odalisque saw she was not to be included in his departure. She noted the luxurious appointments of the house, so different from the threadbare and seedy furnishings of Mr. Middleton's one lone room, but rather a thousand times would she have been there. A tumult of yearning and love filled her heart, but beyond the slow tears in her eyes and the trembling lips, no one could have guessed it. Once more she was a Moslem slave, sold by the man whom last night she had thought——She bowed to kismet and strangled her feelings as she had so many times before. And so after a shake of the hand, Mr. Middleton left her, left her to learn as the idol of Mr. Crayburn's life, with every whim gratified, that the first American she had known was but one of millions.

Away toward Englewood hastened Mr. Middleton, reasoning with himself in a somewhat casuistical manner. His conscience smote him as he thought of the previous night. But what else could anybody have done? Deprived of the power of communicating by the means of words, he had by caresses assuaged her grief and stilled her fears and now it was too plain he had made her love him and he had left her in desolation. But heigho! what was the use of repining over spilled milk and nicotined fingers that another man and good would care for, and he himself had not been unscathed by Cupid's darts there the night before.

The young lady of Englewood was just putting on her hat to go out and was standing before the mirror in the hallway. Mr. Middleton had never called at that hour of the day. For months he had not called at all and she never expected that he would again. So without any apprehension at all, she was wearing one of the green silk shirt waists she had made from the Turkish trousers he had given her, and had just got her hat placed to suit her, when there he was!

She turned, blushing furiously. Whether it was the confusion caused her by being discovered in this shirt waist, or the joy of seeing him again and the complete surrender, she made in this joy, so delectable and unexpected and which was not unmixed with a little fear that if he went away this time, he would never come back again, never! whether it was these things or what not, she made no struggle at all as Mr. Middleton threw his arms about her, threw them about her as if she were to rescue him from some fate, and though he said nothing intelligible for some time, but kissed her lips, cheeks, and nose, which latter she had been at pains to powder against the hot sun then prevailing, she made no resistance at all and breathed an audible "yes," when he uttered a few incoherent remarks which might be interpreted as a proposal of marriage.

Here let us leave him, for all else would be anti-climax to this supreme moment of his life. Here let us leave him where I wish every deserving bachelor may some day be: in the arms of an honest and loving woman who is his affianced wife.

Milton Keynes UK
Ingram Content Group UK Ltd.
UKHW030908151124
451262UK00006B/909